The Hamlyn Book of

horror

Daniel Farson

HAMLYN ·
London · New York · Sydney · Toronto

First published by Hamlyn as a Beaver
paperback in 1977
This hardback edition first published in 1979
by The Hamlyn Publishing Group Limited
London · New York · Sydney · Toronto
Astronaut House, Feltham, Middlesex, England
Second impression 1980

© Copyright Text Daniel Farson 1977, 1979

© Copyright illustrations The Hamlyn
Publishing Group Limited 1979

ISBN 0 600 34558 0
Printed in Italy

Contents

A Word of Warning

Do not be alarmed by these stories.

To one person a snake is horrible, to another a spider — but just think, as they slide and scuttle away, how horrible we must seem to them!

Nothing is more horrifying than a sudden shadow at midnight, yet a heartbeat later you realise it was only a trick of moonlight.

So if some of these tales strike you as too horrible to bear, remember it is all in the mind. The living-death lethargy of the Zombies was probably induced by drugs and the Black Dog of Death was probably a labrador.

Everything has an explanation. Or has it?

Come to think of it, there are creatures that defy the imagination — such as werewolves and vampires.

Perhaps it *would* be just as well to look under your bed before you turn out the light tonight! Who knows *what* you will find!

Of Ghosts and Ghouls

'As I was going up the stair
I met a man who wasn't there.
He wasn't there again today.
I wish, I wish he'd stay away.'

Hughes Mearns

The pilot who saw the future

Frank Smyth, editor of *Man, Myth and Magic* and *Modern Witchcraft* (1971) and author of *Ghosts and Poltergeists* (1976) knows what he's talking about when it concerns the supernatural.

Frank Smyth. His fascinating book, Ghosts and Poltergeists, *includes some bizarre accounts of the supernatural.*

The most impressive 'true' ghost story he has come across is the following, and the ghost is no transparent figure in a white nightie, but a wing commander in the last war.

Wing Commander George Potter was a squadron leader at a Royal Air Force base in Egypt, which sent out bombers to drop mines in the sea-routes of Rommel's supply ships. They operated at night and flew during a 'bomber's moon' – when the full moon reflected on the water helped them to navigate the Mediterranean. Between flights they tried to enjoy themselves drinking, smoking and talking.

One evening Potter entered the mess with Flying Officer Reg Lamb for a nightcap, and looked around to see who else was there. He noticed another wing commander, called Roy, who was surrounded by friends.

Potter and Lamb finished their drinks, when there was a burst of laughter from Roy's corner and Potter turned round:

'Then I saw it. I turned and saw the head and shoulders of the wing commander moving ever so slowly in a bottomless depth of blue-blackness. His lips were drawn back from his teeth in a dreadful grin; he had eye-sockets but no eyes; the remaining flesh of his face was dully blotched in greenish, purplish shadows, with shreds peeling off near his left ear.

'I gazed. It seemed that my heart had swollen and stopped. I experienced all the storybook sensations of utter horror. The hair on my temples and the back of my neck felt like wire, icy sweat trickled down my spine, and I trembled slightly all over. I was vaguely aware of faces nearby, but the horrible death mask dominated the lot.'

Gradually he realised that Flying Officer Lamb was tugging at his sleeve.
'What the hell's the matter?' he asked, 'You've gone as white as a sheet . . . as if you've seen a ghost!'

'I have seen a ghost,' said Potter. 'Roy has the mark of death on him.'
Lamb looked over, but Roy seemed perfectly normal to him. But Potter was still shocked, especially as he knew that Roy would be flying the following night. He wondered if he should go to the group captain with such a story, in the hopes that Roy would be grounded, but decided against such an action. He said later, 'I am convinced that the decision not to interfere was part of a preordained sequence of events.'

11

He waited for news throughout the next night. At dawn the telephone rang with the news that Roy and his crew had been shot down, but the plane had ditched safely and the crew had been spotted clambering into a life raft. Potter felt an enormous sense of relief but it was short-lived. Though they searched for them afterwards, Roy and his crew were never seen again. Then Potter knew what he had seen: the blue-black nothingness was the Mediterranean Sea at night, and he was floating somewhere in it, dead.

Frank Smyth concludes the story, 'The vivid, accurate details of the terrible vision suggest that Potter had, for a moment, been able to look into the future.'

Man with a coffin

This story has been collected by Peter Underwood, President of the Ghost Club, and is the basis for many similar ghost stories.

The episode took place in 1890 in an Irish country house called Tullamore, not far from the sea port of Wexford. It concerns Lord Dufferin, a distinguished man and a former Viceroy of India. Not the man to be scared of ghosts; he was a soldier, cool and self-possessed. His grandson stated later, 'The story is perfectly true, but my grandfather could never explain it . . . because he did not believe in ghosts.'

After spending an enjoyable evening at a friend's house-party in Tullamore, Lord Dufferin went up to his bedroom. He felt at peace with the world, there was a comforting wood fire in the grate and he decided to read a little before going to sleep. After half an hour, he felt curiously restless and put the book down. Then he dozed fitfully.

Usually Lord Dufferin slept well, but at two o'clock he got out of bed and crossed to the window. It was a cloudless night with a full moon (always a full moon in such stories!) and everything was still. Then, suddenly, something caught his eye and he watched fascinated as a figure stepped out from the shadows and walked slowly across the park carrying a large box on his back. He stopped when he was opposite the bedroom window and stared up at Lord Dufferin. The moon lit the man's face –

their eyes met – Lord Dufferin moved back instinctively. He described the man's face later as 'full of horror and malevolence'. As the man turned away and disappeared, Lord Dufferin realised that the box he was carrying was a coffin. The house was as quiet as death and he returned to bed.

When he came down to breakfast the next morning, Lord Dufferin told everyone about his adventure. They had a good laugh and his friend assured him that the house had no history of a ghost. Sure enough, on further visits Lord Dufferin slept in the same bedroom and nothing happened.

And that was all? No. A year later, when he had been appointed Ambassador to France, Lord Dufferin waited at the lift of a Paris hotel where he was going to address a conference on the fifth floor. The lift came down, the doors opened, people came out and others went in, including Lord Dufferin, who was busy in conversation. Suddenly he looked up and noticed the liftman. He stepped back appalled. It was the face he had seen in Ireland, the face of the man who carried the coffin on his back. He waved the lift away and the doors closed.

A few moments later, as it reached the fifth floor, there was a sharp noise followed by a dreadful crash which shook the hotel. The suspension cable had snapped and the lift had plunged to the bottom of the shaft, killing five of the people in it, including the liftman.

Who was the liftman? Lord Dufferin wanted to know, but, curiously enough, no one could tell him. He had replaced the regular liftman only that morning. The hotel had no idea who he was and never discovered where he came from.

Yet, by some strange trick of time, he had saved Lord Dufferin's life.

The sailors with the animal heads

One of the most extraordinary, though little known, Irish ghost stories unearthed by Peter Underwood took place in a small house beside the River Suir in County Waterford.

Appropriately it happened at midnight on Christmas Eve. Eli Hayson was going to bed when he was disturbed by the noise of running footsteps along the waterfront outside. Looking out of the window on to the moonlit quay, he saw a young man in a dark jersey and trousers running desperately towards the house.

As he came closer, Eli recognised his twin brother Jack, a sailor who was supposed to be on a ship called the *Thomas Emery* at Cork. He was about to go down and open the door when he noticed several figures following his brother – strangely, they seemed to rise out of the water. He tried to shout a warning but found he could not move and could not speak. His brother reached the door and tried to open it, but the dark figures closed in around him. For a moment Eli saw his brother's face convulsed with fear, and heard the single cry, 'For God's sake, help me!'

At that moment the moon was hidden by a cloud. When it reappeared, everything was peaceful and Eli was able to move at last. He hurried to the door, but as there was no sign of his brother Jack or anyone else he decided he must have had a bad dream.

Two days later, the captain of the *Thomas Emery* sent the bad news – Jack had fallen overboard and drowned. Apparently he had been sleep-walking. At the inquest in Cork, Jack's father testified he had never known his sons to walk in their sleep, but members of the crew swore they had seen Jack leave his bunk and walk around the ship at night. A verdict of 'Found Drowned' was returned, though the family refused to believe the story.

15

Many years later, Eli was drinking in his favourite pub in Cork when the landlord told him that an old man who lived in the town might be able to tell him something of interest. He finished his drink and walked to the address he had been given, where he found an old man called Matthew Webster. When he learned Eli's name he was reluctant to talk, but at last he revealed the secret that his son Tom had told him shortly before his death two months earlier. It concerned an incident witnessed twenty years before, on a Christmas Eve. Tom had been warming himself by a fire on the quayside when he heard footsteps. Looking up he saw three horrifying figures walking stealthily along the water's edge. They had the bodies of men in sailors' clothes, but their heads were those of animals – apes and a stag.

Though he was terrified, he was curious, too, and crept after them. They went down some steps and rowed off in a dinghy, boarding a schooner moored in the harbour. Tom took another boat and followed, climbing up to the stern of the ship where he hid among some barrels.

His blood turned cold when, from his hiding place, he heard loud groans and shrieks of terror. Suddenly a young man leapt out of the companionway and raced across the deck, pursued by the sinister men with the animal heads.

It was a moonlit night and Tom could see the fear on the young man's face as he ran past, screaming: 'For God's sake, help me!' Tom rushed forward impulsively, but the young man jumped overboard. He was about to dive in after him when the creatures seized him. It was now that Tom discovered they were not a figment of his imagination, but men wearing masks. It was all an elaborate plot by three members of the crew to frighten the young man to death – and they succeeded. Two of them wanted to kill Tom also, but the third was prepared to spare him if he promised to keep quiet. Listening to their threats of what would happen if he breathed a word of what he had seen, Tom swore a solemn oath to say nothing. But the young man's face haunted him, and he told his father about the incident when he was dying.

Eli asked the old man if he knew the date when this happened. Matthew Webster took a pocket book from a chest of drawers – needless to say, the date was the same as the Christmas Eve when Eli 'saw' his brother Jack at the door of their house.

Ghosts are frequently seen by a close relative at the moment of death, and there is a particular affinity between identical twins. A few years ago a newspaper reported the true case of one twin dying at sea and his brother, thousands of kilometres away, dying at the same moment on land – a moment of acute stress shared by someone exceptionally close.

At the moment of Jack's death, pursued by his enemies, it seems quite possible that his twin brother would have felt and seen something.

The curse of the stolen sacrum

Peter Underwood, to whom this book is dedicated, believes he has heard more true ghost stories than any man alive. He believes the following to be the most convincing ghost story of all, and this account is based on his version.

In 1936, Sir Alexander Seton, 10th Baronet of Abercorn and Armour-bearer to the Queen, set sail for Egypt with his wife Zayla. They visited the usual places – the Temple at Luxor and the tomb of Tutankhamun. When their guide showed them around the Great Pyramid, he told them of a tomb that was being excavated nearby and offered to take them there. After making their way down thirty rough stone steps, they entered a room where a crumbling female skeleton was laid out on a stone slab.

Edinburgh is famous for its beautiful 18th century buildings. This photograph was taken about the same time as Sir Alexander Seton's strange experiences in Egypt and later in Edinburgh.

Back in their hotel that night, Lady Seton showed her husband a bone she had taken away with her when she slipped back, unnoticed, for a final look. 'It looked like a digestive biscuit,' wrote Sir Alexander. In fact it was the sacrum, a triangular bone connecting the base of the spine with the pelvis.

Safely home in Edinburgh, the Setons told their friends of their journey and showed them the Bone which Sir Alexander kept in a glass case on a corner table in the dining-room. Strange incidents then began to occur – so strange that Sir Alexander began to wonder if he was under a curse for possessing the stolen sacrum. As his guests left the house, a huge piece of the roof came crashing down within a metre of him. The next morning a chimney blew off, but as there was a strong wind at the time Sir Alexander did not take

'"It looked like a digestive biscuit," wrote Sir Alexander. In fact it was the sacrum, a triangular bone connecting the base of the spine with the pelvis.'

this too seriously. However, a few nights later, the children's nanny burst into his bedroom to say she heard someone moving about in the dining-room below. When he went down everything seemed all right, though he thought he heard a crash later on. Finding the corner table overturned the next morning, with the glass case on the floor, his wife was sure he must have upset it in the night without realising it. Sir Alexander knew he had not, but thought it could have overturned because of the vibration from traffic outside.

From then on, all sorts of curious things were heard and seen. A nephew saw 'a funny-dressed person going down the stairs', servants were alarmed by a 'spectral robed figure wandering about the house at night', and some of them gave notice and left. By now, Sir Alexander was alarmed too. He took the sacrum to the drawing-room upstairs, locked the doors and windows, and kept watch outside on the balcony. Nothing happened, so after waiting there several hours he went to bed. Almost at once, so it seemed, his wife woke him up shouting that someone was moving about in the drawing-room. Seizing his revolver, he met the nanny in the passage, also woken by the noises. Unlocking the door, he found the room had been broken into – '. . . it looked as if a battle royal had taken place' – with chairs and books thrown all over the place. The Egyptian Bone, however, remained where he had put it.

Sir Alexander checked the windows, but there was no way anyone could have entered. A short period of comparative peace followed, apart from two mysterious fires and the sound of bangs and crashes which the family was now used to. All too soon the room was disturbed again, more violently this time, with ornaments broken, glass smashed, and '. . . even the table on which the Bone stood seemed to have been subjected to some kind of severe pressure for one leg was cracked.'

A Scottish newspaper heard of the story and published the headline:

*BARONET FEARS
PHARAOH CURSE ON FAMILY*

One of the reporters borrowed the Bone for a few days, but nothing happened. Two weeks later he collapsed and had to have an emergency operation.

The Bone was returned to the Seton's drawing-room, and soon after, the nanny heard another tremendous crash – it was found on the floor, broken into five pieces. Various suggestions were made: that Lady Seton should return to Egypt and replace the Bone in the tomb (she wouldn't hear of that), or that it should be buried or thrown into the sea. Sir Alexander refused to sell the thing, afraid of what might happen to anyone who bought it.

Meanwhile, Lady Seton had taken the sacrum to a doctor, who put the pieces together, and it was restored to the house and placed on a table in the hall. One evening, during a dinner party, both the table and the Bone were hurled across the hall, striking the dining-room wall with such violence that the maid fainted, a cousin swooned, the guests became hysterical and the dinner was spoilt. It was time to get rid of the Bone. While his wife was away, Sir Alexander asked his uncle, Father Benedict of the Abbey at Fort Augustus, to perform an exorcism. The Bone was blessed, then it was burnt until no trace of it was left.

Vampires

'Rubbish Watson, rubbish!
What have we to do with walking
corpses who can only be held in their
graves by stakes driven through
their hearts? It's
pure lunacy.'

(The Adventures of the Sussex Vampire
by Sir Arthur Conan Doyle)

Are there such things?

A vampire is someone who is between life and death. Count Dracula was described as one of the 'undead'. A vampire is the creature of the night. When the sun sets he becomes active, and after climbing out of his coffin he assumes the shape of a living person. But at the first sign of daylight he has to return to his coffin, where he lies motionless, as if dead.

Anyone, male or female, is in danger of becoming a vampire once bitten, for this is how the vampire survives – by sucking the blood of the living. So the idea of the vampire as a thin, white-faced creature is wrong. On the contrary, after a feast of blood the vampire will be fat and rosy-cheeked.

How do you recognise a vampire? There are so many theories that almost anyone can be mistaken for a vampire – those born on Christmas Day, seventh sons of seventh sons, anyone with eyebrows that join, red hair or blue eyes – all are suspect! This is fantasy, of course, but if you meet someone who has no reflection or shadow, then you should be worried – vampires cannot be seen in glass and cast no shadow.

How can you protect yourself? Remember that the vampire is terrified by two things – garlic, and a crucifix or anything in the shape of a cross. How do you destroy a vampire?

The actor, Christopher Lee, in his famous role as Dracula. He is seen here in Hammer Films' 1958 version of Dracula *directed by Terence Fisher.*
Inset: Here are the two things which will always protect you from vampires – garlic and a crucifix.

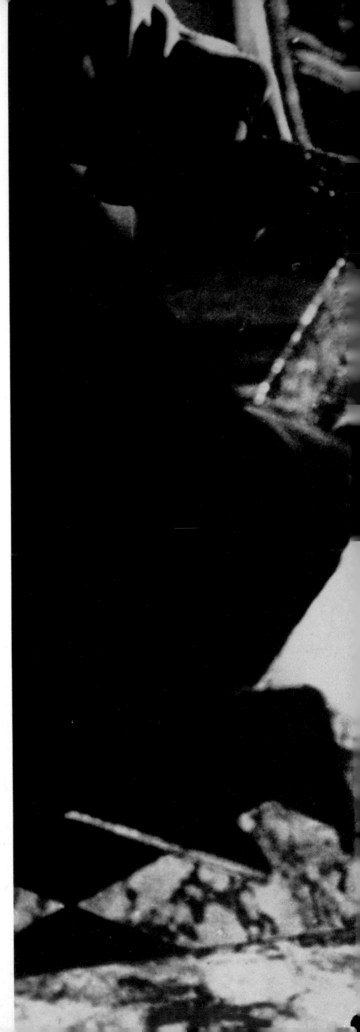

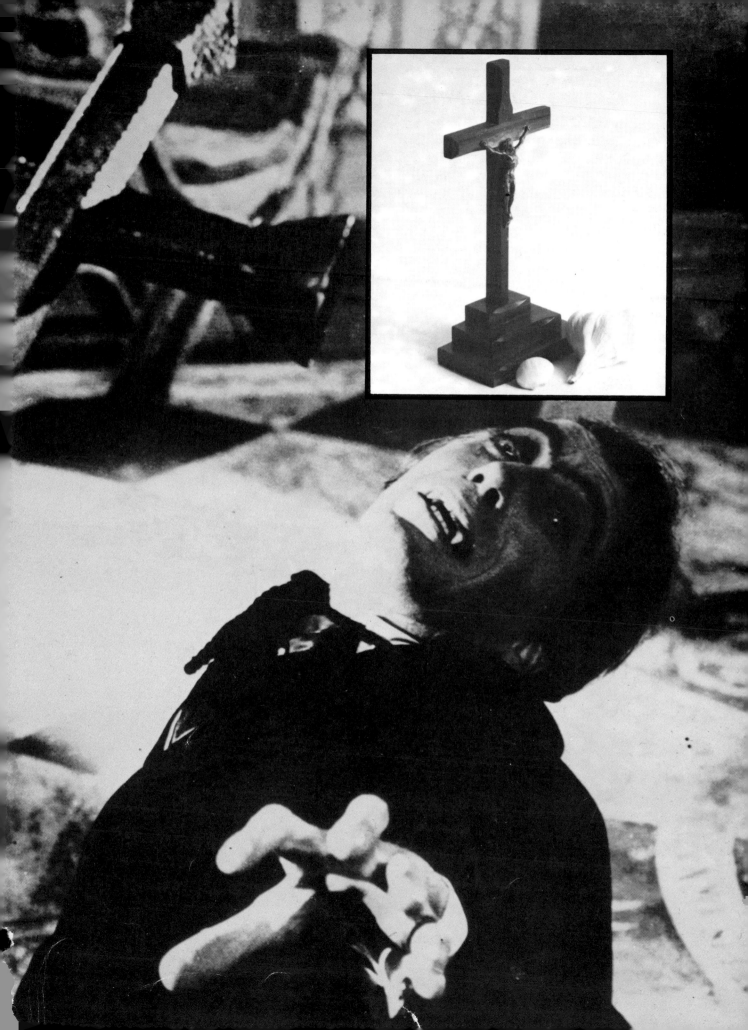

First catch him, preferably when he is lying inside his coffin. Then it is necessary to hammer a wooden stake straight through his heart with a single blow. If you find this too horrific (and who can blame you?) then remember that the vampire can also be destroyed by the light of day. If you meet him after dawn, open the curtains or force him into the sunlight and he will turn to dust. If he has become a wolf, he can only be killed by a silver bullet.

So, do vampires really exist? On the face of it, few beliefs could be sillier – that dead people should rise from their graves at night to suck the blood of the living – yet people have believed in vampires since the beginning of time.

Montague Summers. This extraordinary man was a clergyman who lived from 1880–1948 and became one of the world's most famous experts on the history of vampires.

The true stamping ground – or gliding ground – of the vampire is Eastern Europe; Austria, Hungary, Yugoslavia and Romania. Romania was split into three states until the First World War – Wallachia, Moldavia and Transylvania.

A clergyman called Montague Summers, one of the most famous experts on the history of the vampire, has written, '. . . in Romania we find gathered together around the vampire almost all the beliefs and superstitions that prevail throughout the whole of Eastern Europe.'

He mentions superstition – is this all there was to it? Certainly this is just what we should expect in remote parts of the 'land beyond the forest', infested by wolves, where people were darkly ignorant. It's hardly surprising if they were superstitious. A typical story is that of the young soldier returning home from war, who meets a girl as he walks beside the lake close to his village. She is pale, dark-haired and beautiful. They talk, and suddenly he notices that though he can see his own reflection in the water there is no one beside him. He falls, fainting, and when he recovers he really is alone. Arriving home he tells everyone of his meeting with the girl, only to be greeted with cries of horror – she had died several weeks earlier.

But there have been cases of vampirism officially witnessed and recorded by magistrates, priests and army officers, who should have known better than to believe in 'old wives' tales'. In 1732 a deputation was sent from Belgrade to investigate the report of a vampire who was attacking a family in a remote village in Yugoslavia. They were distinguished men – civil and military officials, a Public Prosecutor, various 'respected persons', twenty-four soldiers and a lieutenant of the Prince of Wurtemberg. They discovered that a man who had died three years before had returned as a vampire and killed three of his nieces and nephews and one brother in the last fortnight. He had started to suck the blood of his fifth victim, a beautiful niece, when he was interrupted and escaped.

As darkness fell the deputation went to the man's grave, followed by a crowd of frightened villagers. When they opened his coffin he looked as healthy as anyone there – his hair, his fingernails, his teeth, and even his eyes (which were half-open) were all intact. One detail of this story is mentioned casually, but is sensational – the man's heart was still beating. When they pierced it with an iron bar, a white fluid burst out, mixed with blood. Then they cut off his head with an axe and buried his body in quicklime, after which the last girl who had been attacked began to recover.

The British vampire

The best-known British vampire lived in Cumberland at Croglin Grange, according to the story told by a Captain Fisher to the writer Augustus Hare. No one seems to know of a Croglin Grange today, but there is a farmhouse called Croglin Lower Hall, not far from the churchyard, and Croglin can be found on the map. It means 'crooked river' – a perfect description for Croglin Water, which flows round Watch Hill.

Captain Fisher said the Grange, which overlooked the nearby church, was rented by two brothers and their young sister. One night as she lay in bed she glimpsed something moving across the lawn in the moonlight. A few moments later she was horrified to hear the sound of scratching at her window, and then she saw a brown figure with flaming eyes behind the glass. With long, bone-like fingers 'it' tried to take out a leaded window pane, while she watched, too frightened to move. When a pane fell out 'it' reached inside and unlocked the window. The creature dragged the girl's head over the bed and sank its teeth into her throat as she started to scream. Her brothers came running when they heard the noise, to find their sister unconscious and bleeding while the creature escaped.

In order to recover from the shock, they took the girl to Switzerland for a holiday. When they returned to the house, at her insistence, everything seemed peaceful enough, but one winter's night she heard that terrible 'scratch, scratch, scratch' on her window again. As she saw the same 'hideous brown face' she screamed, and this time her brothers saw the creature scrambling across the lawn, and fired, shooting 'it' in the leg. The next day they followed a trail of blood to a family vault in the churchyard, and discovered that all the coffins except one had been broken into. When this was opened, they saw 'it' – brown and mummified, the same hideous face that had looked through the window, with a bullet in its leg.

Vampires today

The idea of vampires is hard to accept even in darkest Transylvania in the middle of the eighteenth century, so it seems incredible that they should be 'alive' and 'biting' now.

Yet there are startling 'cases' even in the twentieth century. In New York, this experience was reported by a girl called Lillith. She told two psychic researchers that she had gone to a cemetery, where a young man tried to kiss her. It is not too clear what she was doing there, but suddenly she became possessed by a surge of strength and plunged her teeth into the man's neck, drawing blood. 'I never considered myself a Dracula,' she said, 'but rather a very evil person who liked the taste of blood.'

In 1974 a Romanian woman, called Tinka, told me of her father's death when she was a girl. His body was laid out in the traditional way, but when the family tried to lift his legs to fit him in the burial clothes, they discovered that 'rigor mortis' had not set in and his limbs were soft. In fact 'rigor mortis' is only a temporary state, but they were so horrified that the story spread rapidly through the village – they had a vampire in their midst!

So what did they do? Perhaps you can guess – the villagers marched to the house, tore off the sheet that covered the corpse, and plunged a wooden stake through the man's heart.

Inset: Dennis Wheatley, 1897–1977, the master of the occult. After a varied and successful business career, Dennis Wheatley started writing in 1932. Since then his work has been translated into 31 languages. He is chiefly remembered for those novels which had a flavour of witch-craft and the occult, although he wrote detective stories and historical adventure stories which introduced his attractive hero, Roger Brook.

Simple explanations

Without wishing to pour cold water (or garlic juice!) on the idea of the vampire, there are a number of simple reasons which explain the legend. Dennis Wheatley, author of such thrillers as *The Devil Rides Out*, has a convincing theory that in times of extreme poverty beggars would make their homes in graveyards, emerging from tombs in the cover of darkness to scavenge for food. If they were seen in the moonlight, stealing out of coffins, it is not very

surprising that rumours would be spread quickly by word of mouth from person to person, then from village to village, until the seeds of the legend would be sown over an entire district.

There is another obvious theory which explains a great deal – that vampires were really unfortunate people who had been buried alive. Premature burial has taken place on occasions right up to the present day, for the simple reason that a state of death is extremely difficult to certify. In 1885, the *British Medical*

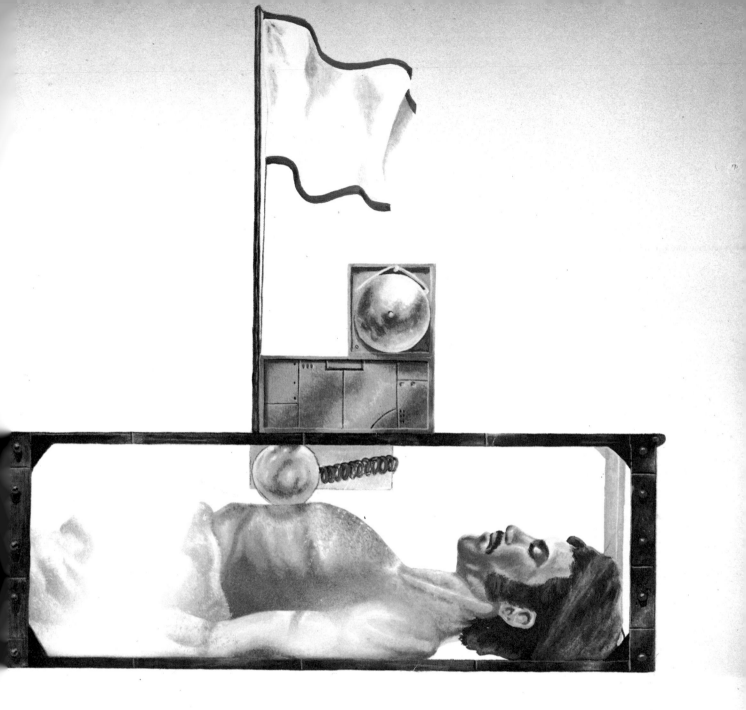

Journal stated, 'It is true that hardly any one sign of death, short of putrefaction can be relied on as infallible.' This is just as true today – for without sophisticated clinical tests, you can only really be certain that death has occurred when the body begins to decay. In fact, you can still occasionally read of the terrible shock that befalls an unlucky mortuary attendant when he finds that one of his corpses is still alive.

A number of Victorians were terrified of being buried alive. Wilkie Collins, who wrote two of the first and most famous thrillers – *The Moonstone* and *The Woman in White* – left instructions for various tests to be made before he was buried, so that there should be no doubt that he was dead. A Russian, Count Karnicki, invented a coffin with a glass ball resting on top of the body. If the corpse moved, the ball released a spring and the lid would fly open while a flag waved above and a bell rang for assistance. This contraption sounds pretty silly, but Collins and Karnicki had a point when you consider that at least one person was buried alive every week in America at the beginning of this century!

One such victim was a young woman who lived near Indianapolis. When she collapsed, six doctors signed the death certificate after making the usual tests, but her young brother refused to believe them. He tried to prevent her body being removed for the funeral several days later, and in the struggle a bandage came loose round her jaw and it could be seen that her lips were moving.

'What do you want, what do you want?' cried the boy.

'Water,' she whispered faintly. She revived and lived to an old age.

Another American woman, the respected matron of a large orphanage, was declared dead and her body placed in a shroud before she was rescued and revived by friends. Needless to say, extra precautions were taken the next time she was presumed to be dead, but again her body was shrouded. Luckily, the undertaker happened to pierce her body with a pin, and noticed that a small drop of blood oozed from the puncture, to the joy of her friends who helped her recover. These women were fortunate – just imagine the numbers of people who were not rescued in time. It is a grisly thought.

Earlier in history, there was the case of the Grand Inquisitor of Spain. His heart was revealed while he was being embalmed, and was seen to be beating. At this moment the Cardinal regained consciousness and even tried to reach forward and grasp the embalmer's knife before he sank back and 'died' again.

This incident is echoed horrifically by a case in our own time, of a patient whose kidneys were being removed for a transplant, when it was discovered that the 'corpse' was alive. This happened in Birmingham in 1973. Just think – if we can make such mistakes with all our modern science and medical knowledge, how easy it must have been a few hundred years ago when people did not understand states of trance which look like death. Catalepsy, for example, can make the body go rigid, but it is really a form of suspended animation, and can last for several weeks.

No wonder that a doctor signed a death certificate in Moravia (now part of Czechoslovakia)

when a postman was thought to have died from epilepsy. A few years later, when the bodies had to be removed from this particular graveyard, it was discovered that the postman had been buried alive and had died from suffocation – the guilt-stricken doctor was never the same man again.

Premature burial was once so commonplace in Britain that the Burial Reformer published the following verse:

'There was a young man at Nunhead,
Who awoke in his coffin of lead.
"It is cosy enough,"
He remarked in a huff,
"But I wasn't aware I was dead."'

When the bodies of people who were buried alive were dug up, or disturbed by grave-robbers or body-snatchers, it was discovered that they had moved. Sometimes there might be blood round the mouth where the wretched person had bitten himself in a final agony, and this gave rise to the belief that they were vampires. In some cases there were signs that the shroud had been eaten in a last desperate attempt to stay alive, and although it is more likely that the shroud was devoured by insects, stories can spread like wildfire and grow more fantastic in the telling.

In other words, a belief in vampirism might well have been a form of mass hysteria. This would have been especially likely in times of plague, when people would have been anxious for a scapegoat. Also, there was a natural fear of disease during plague outbreaks and a wish to bury bodies as soon as possible to prevent infection.

When the cholera epidemic swept across Europe at the start of the last century, it reached as far as County Sligo in the west of Ireland. A girl called Charlotte Thornley lived there with her parents. Years later, she remembered two strange incidents – first there was the soldier called Sergeant Callan, who was such a giant of a man that no coffin would hold him after he died from cholera. When an undertaker took a hammer to break his legs, in order to squeeze him in, the Sergeant sprang back to life and Charlotte saw him afterwards walking around, with a limp, presumably!

During the great cholera epidemic that swept across Europe at the beginning of the last century, hasty burials were made in the effort to stop infection. This could result in tragedy when some people were buried alive.

The second case concerned a man whose wife had died after he carried her to the hospital on his back, with a red handkerchief tied round her waist to ease the pain. During this emergency, it was the practice to throw as many as fifty corpses into a trench and cover them with lime, to stop infection. Searching for his wife to give her a proper burial, the man noticed a corner of the red handkerchief, and when he lifted her body, he discovered that she was still alive. 'He carried her home,' Charlotte Thornley remembered, 'and she recovered and lived for many years afterwards.'

By this time Charlotte had grown up and married an Irish civil servant called Abraham Stoker. They had a son called Bram, who was a sickly child and bedridden for the first eight years of his life. His mother's memories of the plague may have been his bedtime stories too, giving him his first taste for horror. Years later, as Bram Stoker, he wrote the greatest vampire story of all – *Dracula* (see chapter 4).

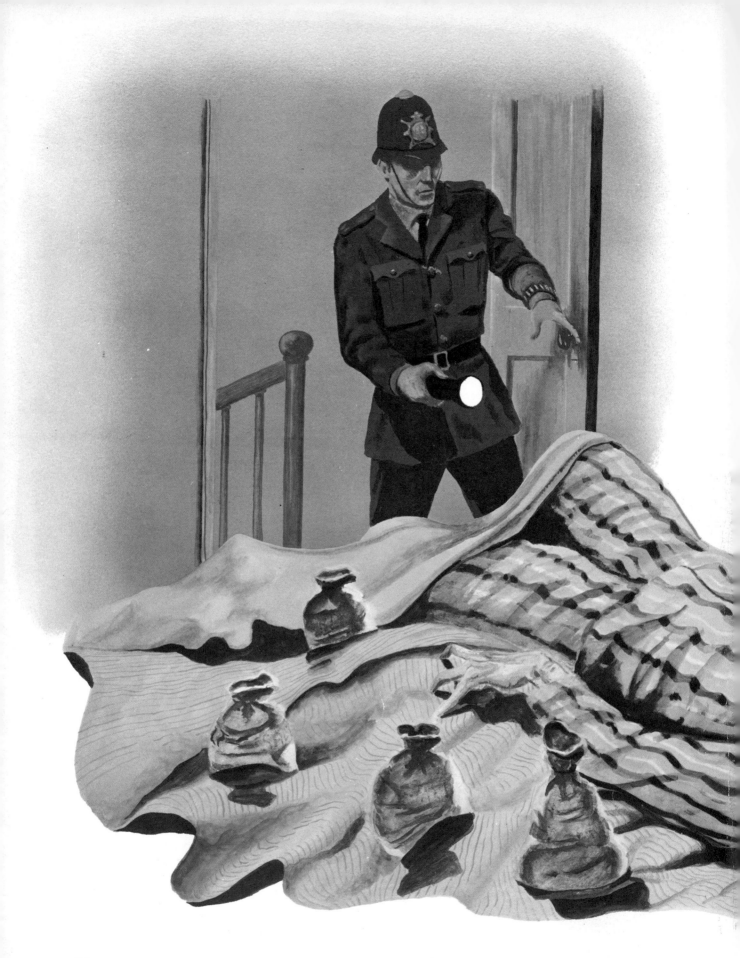

The man in Stoke-on-Trent

Are vampires imaginary? Because people want to believe in something, they are sometimes prepared to believe in anything, but if vampires are nothing more than make-believe, what of official reports by the 'experts in law'?

The great French philosopher Jean-Jacques Rousseau, who lived in the eighteenth century, declared, 'If ever there was in the world a warranted and proven history, it is that of vampires. Nothing is lacking: official reports, testimonials of persons of standing, of surgeons, of clergymen, of judges; the judicial evidence is all-embracing.' Dom Calmet, who did his best to keep an open mind, agreed with Rousseau.

'It seems impossible not to subscribe to the prevailing belief that these apparitions do actually come forth from their graves.' But, as the police would confirm, eyewitnesses may be sincere but they are notoriously unreliable. They are often just as mistaken as the Irish villagers who saw a white lady cross a bridge at midnight – she proved to be a swan! The Croglin Grange vampire is a good story, but is it anything more? Perhaps Tinka's father was not dead when they started to prepare him for the funeral, but simply in a trance and in no danger of becoming a vampire?

It is all too easy to dismiss vampires when you do not believe in them, but to those who do believe, they are terrifyingly real. An extraordinary example is the man who believed he was being attacked by vampires – not in Transylvania in the eighteenth century but in Stoke-on-Trent in 1973! One night in January a young Police Constable, John Pye, was called out to investigate the death of a Pole, Demetrious Myiciura, who worked as a potter and rented a room at Number 3 The Villas – an avenue of large, old-fashioned, rather faded houses.

The room was unusual – for one thing there were no electric light bulbs. As P.C. Pye's flashlight slowly revealed the scene, he suspected he was in a sort of fortress, prepared against attack by vampires. Salt was scattered round the room and sprinkled over the bed, and bags of it lay beside the dead man's face and body. Among other precautions, a bowl containing garlic rested on the window-ledge.

At first the pathologist's report suggested that the man had died from bolting his food, as a pickled onion was found sticking in his throat. However, P.C. Pye had shown the initiative of going to the Public Library and taking out a book called *Natural History of the Vampire* by Anthony Masters, which confirmed his suspicion that salt and garlic are traditional ways of scaring off vampires. The coroner ordered a closer examination and P.C. Pye was proved right – the pickled onion was really a clove of garlic which the man placed in his mouth at night as a final safeguard before going to sleep. He had choked on it and died.

Vampires *did* exist to this man and, in a strange sort of way, they *did* get him in the end. But are there such things? Who knows?

Werewolves

'Does your head become like that of a wolf?'
'I do not know how my head was at the time;
I used my teeth.'

(Cross examination of a 'werewolf' in 1598)

The legend of the werewolf

A werewolf is a man or woman who can change into a wolf. The translation from the early Anglo-Saxon is simple: *wer* means man, *wulf* is wolf. There are three types of werewolf – the true werewolf; the *Iycanthrope* (someone who thinks he is a wolf and behaves like one); and a strange and gruesome third version – a human being who looks ordinary on the outside but whose skin is inside-out. In olden days, hundreds of innocent people were torn apart to see if they were furry inside:

'Two nights since
One met the duke 'bout midnight in a lane
Behind Saint Mark's Church, with the leg
  of a man
Upon his shoulder; and he howled
  fearfully,
Said he was a wolf, only the difference
Was, a wolf's skin was hairy on the outside
His, on the inside!'
(from *The Duchess of Malfi*, by John Webster)

The werewolf and the vampire have much in common. It was generally believed that a werewolf became a vampire after death.

How did people become werewolves? All too easily! If you ate part of a sheep that had been killed by a wolf, or drank water from a wolf's footprints, it was said that you were likely to become a werewolf. Mind you, it is dangerous to eat the flesh of *any* animal killed by a wolf or fox, for you could become infected with rabies or some other disease. If this had happened long ago, and the person foamed at the mouth, he might have been considered a wolf. As for drinking from a wolf's footprints, you'd have to be odd to do that in the first place!

How do you recognise a werewolf? If you meet someone who has pointed ears, hair on the palms of his hands, curved fingernails or eyebrows that meet in the middle, you will have to take care! The eyes of a werewolf always stay human.

Basically, belief in werewolves can be explained by the ignorant fear of anyone different. Even so, many people wanted to become werewolves, and were prepared to suffer elaborate rituals to do so. The right moment for the transformation was midnight, by the light of the full moon. It was supposed to help if you smeared yourself with the fat of a newly-killed cat mixed with aniseed, and wore a belt of wolf's skin. In Russia, the would-be wolf knelt inside a circle while the magic potions simmered. He chanted a tribute to the wolf spirit:

'Make me a werewolf strong and bold
The terror alike of young and old.
Grant me a figure tall and spare;
The speed of the elk, the claws of the bear;
The poison of snakes, the wit of the fox;
The stealth of the wolf, the strength of
  the ox;
The jaws of the tiger, the teeth of the
  shark;
The eyes of a cat that sees in the dark.'

Don't bother to try this (it won't work!). It was supposed to conjure up a tall phantom-like figure which glowed in the darkness until it assumed the form of 'a tall thin monstrosity, half human and half animal, grey and nude with very long legs and arms, and the feet and claws of a wolf.' From then on, the man or woman became a werewolf at sunset and returned to human shape at dawn by rolling in the dew. This continued until death or until the werewolf was shot by a silver bullet. Then the body had to be buried, never burnt.

All this was primitive superstition. Reports of werewolves were most common in wild regions where the wolf was feared as a dangerous animal. As cities spread into the countryside, werewolves started to disappear. Werewolves fitted neatly into ancient folklore – a good tale for the fireside on long winter nights when there was little else to talk about, apart from the wild animals of the forest and the wilder characters in the villages. Just as London cockneys warned their children not to wander in the East End streets after dark, after the murders of 1888 ('or Jack the Ripper will get you'), it was natural for peasants to threaten their children: 'Don't go out in the woods tonight or a werewolf will gobble you up.' True enough – a real wolf might!

So, are there such things as werewolves? Surprisingly, a number of people have taken the legend seriously. In the *Book of Werewolves*,

Being an account of a Terrible Superstition
(1865), Sabine Baring-Gould said the legend
was so persistent, 'everywhere and in all ages,
it must rest upon foundation of fact.' He even
claimed, 'Half the world believes, or believed
in werewolves'.

Like vampirism, reports of werewolves have
been noted since earliest times. Ovid, the
Roman poet (43 B.C. to A.D. 17?), wrote of a king
who was transformed by the gods:

'In vain he attempted to speak; from that
very instant his jaws were bespluttered
with foam, and he thirsted for blood, as he
raged amongst flocks and panted for
slaughter. His vesture was changed into
hair, his limbs became crooked; a wolf,
yet he retained traces of his ancient
expression. Hoary as he was before, his
countenance rabid, his eyes glittered
savagely, the picture of fury.'

The reference to his 'rabid' appearance is in-
triguing, suggesting that the man was suffering
from a form of rabies.

One of the classic werewolf stories is told by

*Left: Legends of werewolves were rife where wolves
roamed free. In this French engraving, the werewolf,
unharmed by a spear, carries off a girl to her doom.
Above: Another representation of a werewolf, from an
18th century engraving.*

Petronius, a Roman of the first century A.D.,
whose account has a universal theme. A servant accompanied a soldier one night on a journey out of town. He was aghast to see the
soldier strip off his clothes by the roadside and
change instantly into a wolf. With a howl, the
creature leapt into the woods and the servant
picked up the clothes, only to find they had
turned into stone. Continuing to his destina-
tion, the servant was told that if he had arrived
a moment earlier he could have helped in fighting off a wolf which had broken into the farm
and killed cattle until driven away by a man
with a sword, which he had thrust into the
animal. Hurrying back home, the servant came
to the place where the soldier's clothes had
been left – now there was only a pool of blood.
At home he found the soldier, wounded by a
sword-thrust, with a surgeon dressing his
neck.

'He took the wolf's paw, which he had put in his pouch as a trophy, but to his amazement it was no longer a paw but a delicate female hand.'

This sort of story has echoed through the ages. In 1558, a hunter in the French forests of the Auvergne met a nobleman who asked him to bring him some game if he was lucky. Later, the hunter was attacked by a savage wolf but was able to drive it away after slashing off one of its paws. Returning home, he remembered his friend and called at his château to tell him of the adventure. At the end of his story he took out the wolf's paw, which he had put in his pouch as a trophy, but to his amazement it was no longer a paw but a delicate female hand. The nobleman started back, recognising the gold ring on one of the fingers. He raced upstairs to find his wife bandaging the bleeding stump of her wrist. She confessed to being a werewolf and was burnt at the stake.

Just as Transylvania was the home of the vampire, central France was famous for *loups garoux*, as the werewolves were known. As many as 30,000 cases were listed between 1520 and 1630. Many of these came to trial. On 13th September, 1573, the Parlement at Dole authorised a werewolf hunt after several local children disappeared:

'And since he has attacked and done injury to some horsemen, who kept him off only with great difficulty and danger to their persons, the said court has permitted those who are dwelling in the said places to assemble with pikes, alberds, and sticks to chase and pursue the said werewolf in every place where they may find or seize him; to tie and to kill, without incurring any penalties.'

It seems extraordinary that no one suspected a real wolf!

Two months later, the werewolf hunters heard the screams of a child and the baying of a wolf. Hurrying to the spot, they found a small girl and thought they recognised a man called Gilles Garnier in the 'wolf' that raced away. When a ten-year-old boy disappeared six days later, they raided the hut of the lonely Garnier, who was known as 'the hermit of St Bonnot', and arrested him and his wife.

Garnier confessed at once. He admitted killing a boy the previous August, and a ten-year-old girl in an orchard. He said he appeared in the form of a wolf and attacked her with his teeth and claws. He enjoyed eating her so much that he brought some of the flesh back for his wife's supper. On this evidence, Garnier was burnt alive on 18th January, 1574.

The case of Jean Grenier

Accused 'werewolves' were surprisingly keen to confess. Obviously, torture helped them on, but sometimes it seemed as if they wanted to. A fourteen-year-old shepherd called Jean Grenier is an interesting example. His crimes took place near Bordeaux, thirty years after those of Garnier and, for what his confession is worth, he admitted to having eaten more than fifty children. He confessed with such pleasure that the crowded courtroom burst into laughter when he described chasing an old woman only to find her flesh 'as tough as leather.' When he lifted a child from its cot, he complained that 'it shrieked so loud it almost deafened me' as he prepared for his first bite. Hardly the stuff to take seriously, but three girls testified against him, and his detailed confession was believed though the judge found the evidence so appalling that he sent Grenier to a higher court.

Grenier was sentenced to be burnt, but by now the case had caused such a stir – with further confessions – that it was sent to an even higher court, where the judge showed surprising common sense. First he recorded Grenier's story: 'When I was ten or eleven years old, my neighbour introduced me to the *Maître de la Forêt* (master of the forest) who gave me a wolf skin. From that time I have run about the country as a wolf.' The judge called in two doctors, who decided that Grenier was suffering from 'a malady called lycanthropy which deceives men's eyes into imagining such things.' The judge gave a wise summing-up, which could explain all the confessions and cases of werewolves:

'The court takes into account the young age and the imbecility of this boy, who is so stupid and idiotic that children of seven and eight years old normally show more intelligence, who has been ill fed in every respect and who is so dwarfed that he is not as tall as a ten year old. . . . Here is a young lad abandoned and driven out by his father, who has a cruel stepmother instead of a real mother, who wanders over the fields, without a counsellor and without anyone to take an interest in him, begging his bread, who has never had any religious training, whose real nature was corrupted by evil promptings, need, and despair, and whom the devil made his prey.'

The boy was spared. He was sent to a monastery which the judge visited seven years later. He found that Grenier was unable to understand the simplest things, but still insisted that he was a werewolf.

43

The beggar werewolf

Another merciful verdict, for those days, was granted to a beggar called Roulet at Angers in 1598. He was found half-naked in some bushes, with long hair, nails like claws, and hands clotted with blood, after a boy's body had been discovered in the woods and a wolf seen racing away.

'I was a wolf,' Roulet confessed to the court.
    'Do your hands and feet become paws?'
    'Yes, they do.'
    'Does your head become like that of a wolf?'
    'I do not know how my head was at the time; I used my teeth.'

He was sentenced to a madhouse, but only for two years.

Merciful verdicts in the courts were rare for those convicted of being werewolves. Primitive fear and superstition, coupled with a lack of understanding, led to horrific sentences being passed on people who were mentally ill. The two stories which follow, where werewolves actually help people, are, therefore, most unusual.

The werewolf and the sea captain

A French sea captain was employed in fighting the Huguenots, Protestants who were being persecuted by Catholics in seventeenth century France, and many of whom fled to England. After a raid his ship filled with water and started to sink in the Rhône estuary. The captain would have drowned, but someone came to his rescue and brought him to shore. Reaching out his hand gratefully, he was horrified to find himself grasping a hairy paw. He fell on his knees, thinking he had been saved by the Devil as a reward for his attacks on the Huguenots.

While the captain asked the forgiveness of God, the wolf waited grimly. He then led him to a house, where he gave him food before locking him in a barred room. The captain saw the dead body of a woman in the corner, and

thought this would be his fate as well. But in the morning the werewolf returned in the shape of a Huguenot clergyman, and explained that the woman was his wife, murdered by the captain's crew when they had raided his village the day before. He continued:

'Yes, I am a werewolf. I was bewitched some years ago by the woman Grenier (that name again) who lives in the forest. I saw you drowning. I saved you . . . you who had been instrumental in murdering my wife and ruining my home. Why? I do not know. Had I preferred a less pleasant death for you than drowning, I could have taken you ashore and killed you. Yet I did not, because it is not my nature to destroy anything.'

The captain was so impressed that he became a champion of the Huguenot cause until the day of his death.

Saved by a werewolf

Nice and romantic and unlikely, yet this story might have a basis of truth. Wolves have always been known as wild killers, but this is untrue. It has been discovered recently that wolves only attack man when they are attacked themselves, and they have often been known to save a man's life. One old story concerns an abbot who drank too much cider at a country fair and was overcome by the sun on his journey home. Half-asleep, he fell off his horse, hitting his head on a stone. He bled so profusely that the scent of blood attracted a pack of wild cats from the forest. A werewolf bounded to his rescue and escorted the drowsy abbot to the monastery. At dawn the werewolf assumed human shape again and turned out to be a churchman who lectured the abbot severely for his conduct the day before and stripped him of all his privileges. A protective werewolf, admittedly, but a bossy one!

What are they really?

Are there logical explanations for werewolves? Yes, of course. One of the most obvious is that werewolves were really children lost in the forest, or left there deliberately, and found by packs of wolves who brought them up with their own cubs, teaching them all the hunting skills of the wild animal (see chapter 6).

Another explanation is even simpler – the *Berserkirs*, gangs of Nordic warriors, profited from the wild reputation of the bear by dressing in his skin ('bear-sark' means bear-skin). They prayed to the spirits of the bear and the wolf in the hope of gaining the animal's strength, and then worked themselves into a state of frenzy as they raided remote villages, howling like wolves. 'Going berserk', a phrase they have given to the language, is defined by the dictionary as a 'murderous frenzy'. It is understandable that ignorant villagers, glimpsing them as they howled in the darkness, dressed in animal skins, might wonder what they were, and talk of them afterwards as half-man, half-animal.

Horror Stories

*'If it scares you to read that
one imaginary person killed another,
why not take up knitting?'*

(Ambrose Bierce, American writer
and master of the macabre)

Some horror stories seem so familiar that people think they have read the book even when they haven't. For instance, how many of you think that 'Frankenstein' is the name of the monster, when it is really his creator, Baron Frankenstein? Did you know that Count Dracula had a white moustache, or that Mr Hyde had rooms in London's Soho?

It would be silly to list the best horror stories in any order, as if it were an ugly contest, but it is fair to claim that the three most celebrated horror books in literature are *Dracula* by Bram Stoker, born in Dublin; *The Strange Case of Dr Jekyll and Mr Hyde* by Robert Louis Stevenson, born in Edinburgh; and *Frankenstein* by Mary Shelley, the wife of the poet.

Count Dracula revives life, Baron Frankenstein creates it, and Dr Jekyll shows the conflict inside us between good and evil. These books deal with universal themes of life and death, which explains their lasting popularity. Their names are better known today than when they were written.

Read the great originals, and discover how different they are from what you imagine.

Frankenstein

Mary Shelley (1797–1851) was only nineteen when she wrote *Frankenstein*, one of the strangest books ever written. The story starts in the form of letters written by a man called Robert Walton to his sister Margaret. He tells her that he has hired a ship at Archangel and is busy collecting a crew to sail her to the North Pole.

The following summer Walton meets Victor Frankenstein in the Arctic wastes of the North Pole. The ship has been closed in by ice on every side, when the crew notice a sledge drawn by dogs, guided by a gigantic figure,

Mary Shelley. A portrait painted by R. Rothwell in 1841.

passing northwards. That night the ice breaks up and a fragment drifts towards the ship the following morning. On it is a sledge, one dog, and a man who is nearly frozen to death. When he has recovered, Captain Walton asks why he has come so far on the ice in so strange a vehicle.

'To seek one who fled from me,' replies the stranger.

'And did the man whom you pursued travel in the same fashion?'

'Yes.'

'Then I fancy we have seen him,' says Walton. This news excites the stranger, but he seems to be suffering terribly.

'That night the ice breaks up and a fragment drifts
towards the ship the following morning. On it is a sledge,
one dog, and a man who is nearly frozen to death.'

He asks the Captain to listen to his story.

Victor Frankenstein (for that is the name of the stranger) was brought up in Switzerland. His parents are devoted to him, and he is a brilliant child. At the age of fourteen he becomes obsessed by the 'secrets of heaven and earth' and the search for an 'elixir of life', which will prolong it indefinitely.

When he is seventeen, Frankenstein goes to the University of Ingolstadt, where he is able to continue his studies. At night he learns about anatomy in 'charnel-houses' or mortuaries and graveyards. At last he is able to announce, 'I succeeded in discovering the cause of generation and life; nay, more, I became myself capable of bestowing animation upon lifeless matter.' He starts to build a frame that will hold his manufactured man, who is to be eight feet tall and proportionately large, constructed from bones he collects from the mortuary, the slaughter-house and the dissecting room of a hospital. Finally, he brings the monster to life:

'Great God! His yellow skin scarcely covered the work of muscles and arteries beneath; his hair was of a lustrous black, and flowing; his teeth of a pearly whiteness; but these luxuriances only formed a more horrid contrast with his watery eyes, that seemed almost of the same colour as the dun white sockets in which they were set, his shrivelled complexion and straight black lips.'

He sees the creature open its eyes ... it breathed hard, and a convulsive motion agitated its limbs.

Frankenstein escapes from the house, rejecting the monster he has created.

Frankenstein meets the monster again in the mountains of Chamonix a year later. By this time, the monster has murdered his young brother, so Frankenstein turns on him, trembling with rage and horror.

'Devil . . . Begone, vile insect! Or rather, stay, that I may trample you to dust!'

The monster makes a poignant plea for friendship: 'Be calm! I entreat you to hear me. . . Have I not suffered enough that you seek to increase my misery?' He reminds him that he is stronger than his creator, but refuses to hurt him. 'Oh, Frankenstein,' he implores him pathetically, 'be not equitable to every other, and trample upon me alone, to whom thy justice, and even thy clemency and affection, is most due. Remember, that I am thy creature; I ought to be thy Adam; but I am rather the fallen angel, whom thou drivest from joy for no misdeed. Everywhere I see bliss, from which I alone am irrevocably excluded. I was benevolent and good; misery made me a fiend. Make me happy, and I shall again be virtuous.' He describes his fate — miserably alone, shunned by man and condemned to wander in the desert mountains and dreary glaciers, and threatens that if he does not receive Frankenstein's friendship, he will make mankind share his wretchedness.

Does Frankenstein agree to the monster's demands? If you want to find out what happens (and plenty does!) read Mary Shelley's novel.

51

Mary Shelley was known as Mary Wollstonecraft Godwin at the time she wrote this novel. Her father, William Godwin, was a famous political philosopher. Her mother, Mary Wollstonecraft, was one of the earliest champions of rights for women, and died a few days after Mary was born on 30th August, 1797. A lonely child, many of her early years were spent in Scotland, near Dundee. She remembered the place later as 'blank and dreary', but at the time she had the freedom to escape into a fantasy world of 'waking dreams', talking to the 'creatures of my fancy'.

Her friendship with the romantic poet, Percy Bysshe Shelley, began when she was only fifteen. He was five years older and married. When she was seventeen, she eloped with Shelley and they travelled through France to Switzerland, spending the summer of 1816 on the shores of Lake Geneva. Their neighbour was Shelley's close friend, the poet Lord Byron.

Lord Byron, a portrait painted in 1818, just two years after Mary Shelley wrote Frankenstein *while she was staying with the poet Shelley near Byron's villa on Lake Geneva.*

While he spent the day hard at work writing, they boated on the lake or walked around it until the weather grew so bad that it kept them indoors. Luckily some books of ghost stories kept them amused, and one day Byron suggested that they should each write their own. The two poets soon gave up, and as for Mary, nothing came into her head, though she tried to think of a story 'which would speak to the mysterious fears of our nature, and awaken thrilling horror – one to make the reader dread to look round, to curdle the blood, and quicken the beatings of the heart.'

'Have you thought of a story?' they asked her when she came down each morning, and she had to say, 'No.'

While the two great poets talked, she listened. One of their conversations concerned a scientific experiment with a piece of Italian 'pasta', like spaghetti, called *vermicelli* (which means 'little worm'), which was placed in a glass case and began to move. This gave Mary her inspiration: 'Perhaps a corpse could be re-animated . . . perhaps the component parts of a creature might be manufactured, brought to-gether, and endued with vital warmth.' That night she was unable to sleep. In a sort of waking dream, she saw, 'with shut eyes, but acute mental vision . . . the pale student of unhallowed arts kneeling beside the thing he had put together. I saw the hideous phantasm of a man stretched out, and then, on the work-ing of some powerful engine, show signs of life, and stir with an uneasy, half vital motion. His success would terrify the artist; he would rush away from his odious handiwork, horror stricken. He would hope that, left to itself, the slight spark of life which he had communicated

The villa Diodati, Lord Byron's house on Lake Geneva. It was here that Mary Shelley decided to write the book which later became known as Frankenstein.

would fade. . . He sleeps; but he is awakened; he opens his eyes; behold the horrid thing stands at his bedside, opening his curtains and looking on him with yellow, watery, but speculative eyes.'

Mary opened her own eyes with terror, and remembered her ghost story. When she came downstairs the next morning, she was able to tell the others, 'I have found it! I began that day with the words, *It was on a dreary night of November*, making only a transcript of the grim terrors of my waking dream.'

The game round the blazing wood fire, when each of them had agreed to write about the supernatural, had become serious. Shelley urged her to write a long novel rather than a short story, and she was the first to admit that, but for him, 'it would never have taken the form in which it was presented to the world.'

She completed *Frankenstein* the following May and it was published in March 1818. At the end of 1816, Shelley's wife died (by committing suicide), and he married Mary on 30th December. But tragedy pursued them, with the deaths of their baby daughter and son. In November 1819 another son was born, and survived, but less than three years later Shelley was drowned at sea off the coast of Italy. His body was burnt in a funeral pyre on the beach near Lerici and his ashes buried in Rome. Mary Shelley wrote other books, but none caused the

sensation of *Frankenstein*. She died in 1851 and is buried at Bournemouth. Like Bram Stoker, the author of *Dracula*, she wrote a story that has become a household name, but she herself is hardly remembered.

The Hunchback of Notre Dame

This story was written in 1831 by the great French novelist Victor Hugo under the original title of *Notre Dame de Paris*. On one level it is a romantic historical novel, set in the great Cathedral of Paris in 1482, but it is also the universal story of Beauty and the Beast.

Though you are urged to read the original
novel, be warned that the hunchback, Quasimodo, does not appear until Chapter Three of
Book Four. He is discovered by Claude Frollo,
the youngest chaplain of Notre Dame, who returns from saying Mass on Quasimodo Sunday
and is shocked to see a group of old women
tormenting a foundling child:

'The poor little imp had a great wart
covering its left eye – the head compressed
between the shoulders – the spine crooked
– the breastbone prominent – and the legs
bowed. Yet it seemed to be full of life. . .
Claude's compassion was increased by this
ugliness; and he vowed in his heart to
bring up this child. . .'

Quasimodo is saved, but fate continues to
pursue him. At the age of fourteen the sound
of the great cathedral bells breaks his eardrums
and he becomes deaf. From then on the outside

world is closed to him, and the cathedral becomes a place to hide in. Ironically, the only thing he can hear is the ringing of the bells:

'This was the only speech that he could hear, the only sound that broke for him the universal silence. He expanded in it, like a bird in the sunshine. All at once the frenzy of the bell would seize him; his look became wild – he lay in wait for the great bell as a spider for a fly, and then flung himself headlong upon it. Now, suspended over the abyss, borne to and fro by the formidable swinging of the bell, he seized the brazen monster by the ears – gripped it with his knees – spurred it with his heels – and redoubled, with the shock and weight of his body, the fury of the peal. Meanwhile, the tower trembled; he shouted and gnashed his teeth – his red hair bristled – his breast heaved and puffed like the bellows of a forge – his eye flashed fire – the monstrous bell neighed panting beneath him. Then it was no longer the great bell of Notre-Dame, nor Quasimodo – it was a dream – a whirl – a tempest – dizziness astride upon clamour – a strange centaur, half-man, half-bell – a spirit clinging to a winged monster. . .'

Unable to hear, hardly able to speak, Quasimodo is persecuted by people who cannot understand him and are frightened by his appearance. At one point he is flogged and placed in the pillory, pelted with stones by the mob until he is only half alive. He calls in vain for water until the beautiful gypsy girl, Esmeralda, makes her way through the crowd and lifts a gourd of water to his parched, deformed lips:

'Then, in that eye, hitherto so dry and burning, a big tear was seen to start, which fell slowly down that misshapen face so long convulsed by despair. It was possibly the first that the unfortunate creature had ever shed.'

Later it is Quasimodo's turn to rescue Esmeralda from the executioner and hide her in his cell high up in the cathedral as Victor Hugo's story builds up to a tremendous climax.

Seeing Double

Have you ever seen your double? Unless you hate yourself, this could be quite a pleasant experience, but it is an idea which has been used by some of the greatest masters of horror to great effect.

Some writers, such as Robert Louis Stevenson, Edgar Allan Poe and Sheridan Le Fanu believed that the double was your *guilty conscience*. This was reflected in their finest horror stories – *The Tell-Tale Heart* (Edgar Allan Poe), *In a Glass Darkly* (Sheridan Le Fanu) and *The Strange Story of Dr Jekyll and Mr Hyde* (Robert Louis Stevenson).

57

Edgar Allan Poe, 1809–1849, was a writer of great and original genius. His stories are weird, wild and fantastic, dwelling by choice on the horrific. Orphaned as a young child, Edgar Allan Poe was adopted by a wealthy merchant. After a youth marred by gambling debts and dissipation, he turned to writing. Dogged by alcoholism, he died in poverty in 1849.

Edgar Allan Poe's 'tales'

Some of Poe's longer stories are very well known because they have been filmed – for example *The Fall of the House of Usher*, and *The Murders in the Rue Morgue*. However, it is fair to claim that his greatest prose is contained in the amazing short stories that reveal his inner turmoil.

William Wilson is a classic example of 'seeing double'. The story is told by William Wilson. There is another boy at his Prep school who has the same name, and the two look so alike that they are considered brothers. They even share the same birth date. The narrator's feelings towards this other Wilson are mixed: '. . . not yet hatred, some esteem, more respect, much fear, with a world of uneasy curiosity.' The only marked difference between them is

that the other Wilson speaks in a very low whisper. He copies the narrator's clothes and way of walking, so irritating to the latter that he tries to shake him off.

The narrator goes to Eton, but he cannot escape the other Wilson. After a wild night, with a secret party in his rooms, he is told that a stranger has called for him. Reeling towards the gates, he is clutched by a familiar figure and a voice whispers – 'William Wilson!' He adds: 'I grew perfectly sober in an instant.'

This righteous alter ego even pursues him to Oxford University. One night he wins a considerable amount of money cheating at cards, when the door bursts open and the other Wilson appears. With his fearful whisper, he urges the other player to examine the cuff of the narrator's left sleeve, where they find some extra cards.

He is ruined. He flees the country, but, 'My evil destiny pursued me' – to Paris – to Rome – always interrupting and wrecking his schemes. At last, coming face to face at a masked ball in Rome, he forces the other Wilson against a wall and plunges his sword, 'with brute ferocity, repeatedly through and through his bosom.'

Now he learns, as the reader has suspected already, that his double is himself. As he steps up to a large mirror, 'in extremity of terror, mine own image, but with features all pale and dabbled in blood, advanced to meet me with a feeble and tottering gait.' It is the other Wilson, but he no longer speaks in a whisper. . . 'I could have fancied that I myself was speaking while he said: "You have conquered, and I yield. Yet henceforward art thou also dead. . . In me didst thou exist – and, in my death, see by this image, which is thine own, how utterly thou hast murdered thyself."'

For the other Wilson was his conscience, trying to protect him from himself.

An illustration by Harry Clarke for William Wilson *from a selection of stories by Edgar Allan Poe. Poe's dissipated way of life caused great distress to his family and his feelings of guilt are reflected in this story.*

'They heard! – they suspected! – they knew! – they were making a mockery of my horror! – this I thought, and this I think. But anything was better than this agony. Anything was more tolerable than this derision!'

The Tell-Tale Heart is as perfect as any short story ever written. It is Poe's masterpiece of horror.

It starts with deceptive quiet, which builds up to the tremendous climax when the narrator is showing the police around the room where he has buried a man under the floorboards. He imagines he hears the beating of his heart, growing louder – and louder.

'They heard! – they suspected! – they *knew*! – they were making a mockery of my horror! – this I thought, and this I think. But anything was better than this agony. Anything was more tolerable than this derision! I could bear those hypocritical smiles no longer! I felt that I must scream or die! and now – again! – hark! louder! louder! louder! *louder!*

'"Villains!" I shrieked. "Dissemble no more! I admit the deed! Tear up the planks! Here, here! – It is the beating of his hideous heart!"'

Yet again, the weight of his guilt is too awful for the conscience to bear.

Edgar Allan Poe (1809–49) was pursued by disaster throughout his life – this is one reason why he was such a master of horror. He wrote as if he was looking over his shoulder at someone or some thing behind him.

He was born in Boston, Massachusetts, on 19th January, 1809. His mother, an English actress, died when he was only two. He was then adopted by a businessman called John Allan, but from the start there was a bitter rivalry between the boy and his wealthy but miserly foster father.

60

When Poe was six, the Allans moved to England and he went to a school at Stoke Newington on the outskirts of London, from 1818 to 1820. There is an echo of London life and his school in some of his later stories (see *William Wilson*), but Poe was essentially American in outlook.

He went to an American university, but Allan removed him because of his debts and put him to work in his business. Poe ran away to Boston, joined the army and reached the rank of Sergeant Major. He was admitted to West Point, the famous military academy, but was dismissed later for deliberate neglect of duty.

Above: An illustration from Edgar Allan Poe's Tales of Mystery in the Rue Morgue.
Right: Robert Louis Stevenson, 1850–1894.

of the Grotesque and Arabesque his only payment was some free copies. When a friend visited him as his wife lay dying, he noted that, 'There was no clothing on the bed . . . the weather was cold and the sick lady had the dreadful chills that accompany the hectic fever of consumption. She lay on the straw bed, wrapped in her husband's great coat, with a large tortoise-shell cat on her bosom. The wonderful cat seemed conscious of her great usefulness. The coat and the cat were the sufferer's only means of warmth.' They could not afford to buy coal.

Poe tried to find escape by losing himself in drink, but when he came to himself again, his guilt was all the greater. Fortunately, for us, he found escape in words as well. He used his private nightmare as the inspiration for his tales of horror. Sadly, he had little need to exaggerate – his own life was just as horrible.

The Strange Case of Dr Jekyll and Mr Hyde

Robert Louis Stevenson (1850–94) owed a lot to Poe and was the first to admit it, praising him not only for the 'loathing and horror' in his work, but also for the 'almost incredible insight into the debatable region between sanity and madness.'

In 1836 he made a startling marriage with his cousin Virginia – she was thirteen. Only six years later she broke a blood vessel when she was singing. She died in January 1847. In contrast to his child bride, he now proposed to several elderly women, but his life was rapidly falling to pieces. By 1849 he was terrified of going mad. In September that year he took a boat to Baltimore to make arrangements for his forthcoming marriage to a widow, Mrs Royster Shelton, who had some money and might have been able to look after him, but he vanished. A week later, his doctor received a note to come and fetch him, and found Poe unconscious and dressed in clothes that did not belong to him. No one knew what had happened. He was taken to hospital where he talked to 'spectral and imaginary objects on the walls.' On 7th October he cried out, 'God help my poor soul,' and died. He was forty.

All his life Poe had been short of money, for his work was not popular. When some of his stories were published in two volumes as *Tales*

Like Poe he was possessed by his conscience, expressed in his masterpiece of horror
– *Dr Jekyll and Mr Hyde*. In spite of illness – or
perhaps because of it, as if he knew that time
was running out – Stevenson worked amazing-
ly hard. *The Strange Case of Dr Jekyll and Mr
Hyde* was written, rewritten and printed as a
'shilling shocker' within ten weeks.

It all started, or so Stevenson claimed, with
a nightmare he had at the very time when he
was searching desperately for a new plot. He
started writing it down immediately. After
three days he had finished 27,000 words. He
read the manuscript to his wife Fanny, who
did not like it. She said he had sacrificed a fine
moral story to a 'magnificent piece of sensa-
tionalism'. After a fierce argument, Stevenson
stalked up to his bedroom, where he had
second thoughts. When he came down, he an-
nounced, 'You are right! I have absolutely
missed the allegory, which, after all is the
whole point of it – the very essence of it!' and
he threw the pages on the fire to avoid the
temptation of revising them. He started again
from scratch and after a further three days
completed the book.

Jekyll grips from the opening page. It starts
with a conversation between two old friends,
Mr Utterson, a lawyer, and Mr Enfield, a 'man
about town'. As they pass the back door of an
imposing house, on one of their evening walks,
Enfield recalls an unpleasant incident he witnessed one night when he saw two figures
ahead of him at this same spot, a short man and
a young girl who was running along the pave-
ment and bumped into him: 'and then came
the horrible part of the thing; for the man
trampled calmly over the child's body and left
her screaming on the ground. It sounds like
nothing to hear, but it was hellish to see.'

Enfield had collared the man and an angry crowd gathered around them, including the child's parents. In order to quieten them, the man went inside the house by the back door and came out a few moments later with a cheque for £100 signed by someone else's name, a name that was highly respected. Enfield reveals the identity of the short man to Utterson – a Mr Hyde – and remarks, 'He is not easy to describe. There is something wrong with his appearance; something displeasing, something downright detestable. I never saw a man I so disliked, and yet I scarce know why. He must be deformed somewhere; he gives a strong feeling of deformity, although I couldn't specify the point. He's an extraordinary looking man, and yet I really can name nothing out of the way.'

Utterson is disturbed. Hyde's name is all too familiar, for his old friend Dr Jekyll had revised his will a few weeks earlier with the strange condition that – 'in case of Dr Jekyll's ''disappearance or unexplained absence for any period exceeding three calendar months,'' the said Edward Hyde should step into the said Henry Jekyll's shoes without further delay. . .'

Utterson is now convinced that Jekyll is somehow under the influence of the evil Mr Hyde. He waits to confront Hyde and learn more about him. At last he sees him heading towards the back door of Jekyll's home. Hyde shrinks back as the lawyer touches him on the shoulder, but at least Utterson now knows what he looks like:

'Mr Hyde was pale and dwarfish . . . he had a displeasing smile . . . and he spoke with a husky, whispering and somewhat broken voice . . . but not all of these together could explain the hitherto unknown disgust, loathing and fear with which Mr Utterson regarded him. . . There *is* something more, if I could find a name for it. God bless me, the man seems hardly human! Something troglodytic, shall we say? . . . O my poor old Harry Jekyll, if ever I read Satan's signature upon a face, it is on that of your new friend.'

As the lawyer returns home, he thinks about Jekyll and gives the reader a hint that the doctor was not always as respectable as he seems, 'He was wild when he was young . . . Ay, it must be that; the ghost of some old sin, the cancer of some concealed disgrace . . .' Finally, he sees Jekyll and tells him outright

that he has been learning about his new friend, Hyde, and does not like what he has heard. Jekyll refuses to discuss Hyde, but makes a promise: 'I will tell you one thing; the moment I choose, I can be rid of Mr Hyde. I give you my hand upon that . . .'

But this is not so easy – Hyde is starting to take over. One morning Jekyll wakes up to discover that the hand resting on the bed-clothes is that of Hyde – they are, of course, one and the same person. Sending a desperate message to his friend Dr Lanyon, to get the vital powders which he must take to change him back, Hyde becomes Jekyll before Lanyon's incredulous eyes. This is the famous transformation which haunts the reader's imagination afterwards in the same way as Frankenstein's creature coming to life or Dracula emerging from his coffin. Dr Lanyon relates:

'He put the glass to his lips and drank at one gulp. A cry followed; he reeled, staggered, clutched at the table and held on staring with injected eyes, gasping with open mouth; and as I looked there came, I thought, a change – he seemed to swell – his face became suddenly black and the features seemed to melt and alter – and the next moment, I had sprung to my feet and leaped back against the wall, my arm raised to shield me from that prodigy, my mind submerged in terror. ''Oh God!'' I screamed, and ''Oh God!'' again and again; for there before my eyes – pale and shaken, and half-fainting, and groping before him with his hands, like a man restored from death – there stood Henry Jekyll.'

The story ends with Dr Jekyll's explanation of Hyde, his double:

'It was on the moral side, and in my own person, that I learned to recognise the thorough and primitive duality of man . . . and from an early date, even before the course of my scientific discoveries had begun to suggest the most naked possibility of such a miracle, I had learned to dwell with pleasure . . . on the thought of the separation of these elements. If each, I told myself, could but be housed in separate identities, life would be relieved of all that was unbearable; the unjust might go his way, delivered from the aspirations and remorse of his more upright twin; and the just could walk steadfastly and securely on his upward path.'

The reader has a sneaking sympathy for Hyde, who is more *fun* than the virtuous Jekyll. At least he is a complete person in his villainy, whereas Jekyll suffers from a lifetime of suppressing the natural instincts he enjoyed as a young man, and pays dearly for his pretence of perfection. Through him, Stevenson attacks the Victorian hypocrisy of men who seemed the height of respectability –

Robert Louis Stevenson with his family and servants at Vailima in Samoa. Stevenson is seated in the centre, on his right is his wife, on his left is his mother.

ideal husbands and fond fathers – but in fact led double lives. Jekyll is in fact as guilty as Hyde. It is a moral story, and the moral can be summed up like this: never try to be someone else; accept yourself as you are, faults and all.

It is generally accepted that Stevenson's *The Strange Case of Dr Jekyll and Mr Hyde* was inspired by a dream, but it is more likely that he drew on personal experience to write the novel, for Stevenson was a Jekyll and Hyde in real life, and tormented by his conscience.

He was born in Edinburgh in 1850 and his family was respectable. However, his father encouraged Robert's writing, and paid for the publication of one of his 'blood-and-thunder' stories when he was only sixteen. At seventeen, Robert joined the Engineering Department of Edinburgh University, where he was considered an eccentric.

Many people tolerated him simply because of his respectable background, but this was the one thing he could not tolerate himself. He did not understand his parents and complained that they did not understand him – 'I never feel so lonely as when I am too much with my father and mother, and I am ashamed of the feelings, which makes matters worse.'

To the dismay of his family, he abandoned engineering and found his escape in the back streets of Edinburgh, fascinated by the smoke and squalor of waterfront pubs and the so-called 'dregs of humanity', invaluable material for his writing. Standards were different then and respectable society pretended that such places and such people did not exist – Stevenson was forced to lead a double life. This could have been a passing phase, easily forgotten, except that Stevenson fell in love with a beautiful young girl called Kate Drummond. They were attracted to each other immediately and planned to marry, but his father was so shocked that he threatened the worst punishment he could think of – to stop Robert's allowance of £12 a year. Stevenson surrendered, and in doing so, condemned Kate to a life of squalor. He never forgave himself.

He went on to write such classics as *Treasure Island* and *Kidnapped*, and released some of his guilt in horror stories such as *Dr Jekyll*.

When he was thirty he married Fanny Osbourne. She was thirty-six, with a daughter of seventeen and a son of eight by a previous marriage. A greater contrast to the unfortunate Kate could hardly be imagined, but his family accepted her as the lesser of two evils even though she was 'grizzled' in appearance and a grandmother. Fanny nursed Stevenson through his constant illness from tuberculosis, but also censored his writing. When he wrote a romantic novel with a heroine based on Kate Drummond, she destroyed the manuscript. After that, he seldom included women in his writing. 'My wife hates and loathes and slates my women,' he wrote to his closest friend. Some of the books he wanted to write would have shocked the public he was gaining and might have been banned by libraries, so she was right to dissuade him, but at the same time, she stopped him from stretching his vivid imagination to the utmost – she tamed his genius.

On his father's death, they moved to America and the healthy mountain air of Colorado. But tuberculosis was hard to cure in those days and Stevenson remained wretchedly ill. He spent the £3,000 left him by his father, in buying a yacht and sailing it to Samoa where he bought

300 acres and made a new home. He became known to the natives as Tusitala, the teller of tales, but in England he was referred to as 'The King of the Cannibal Islands'. He was hard at work on *Weir of Hermiston* when he died on 3rd December, 1894, aged forty-four.

The last photograph of Robert Louis Stevenson taken before his death in 1894.

Dracula

Written by Bram Stoker, this novel was published in 1897. The story takes the form of entries from Jonathan Harker's journal, a young solicitor travelling across Europe towards Castle Dracula in Transylvania. Count Dracula is interested in buying a house outside London and Harker brings the documents of a place that seems suitable, called Carfax.

The opening of Stoker's novel is magnificent. Arriving at the old-fashioned Golden Krone Hotel in Bistritz, Harker finds a letter waiting for him from the Count: 'MY FRIEND – Welcome to the Carpathians . . . At the Borgo Pass my carriage will await you and will bring you to me. I trust that your journey from London has been a happy one and that you will enjoy your stay in my beautiful land. Your friend, Dracula.' It might have been more appropriate if Dracula had signed himself 'Your fiend' rather than 'Your friend', but Harker has no suspicion of danger until the following morning when the landlord's wife implores him not to go. She explains that this is the eve of St George's Day, and that 'when the clock strikes midnight, all the evil things in the world will have full sway.' She begs him to take the crucifix she wears – 'for your mother's sake' – and ties it round his neck.

A crowd has gathered around the carriage outside, and Harker notices that the people cross themselves and point two fingers towards him. A fellow passenger explains that this is a sign to ward off the evil eye.

The carriage reaches the Borgo Pass an hour before midnight, but there is no one waiting to take Harker to Castle Dracula. The driver urges him to continue and return the next day but the horses begin to snort and plunge wildly while he is speaking. A carriage suddenly appears, driven by a tall man with a long brown beard and a great black hat which hides his face.

Harker's luggage is transferred, and he continues his journey to the castle, where the driver disappears. At last the door is opened by the Count:

'"Welcome to my house! Enter freely and of your own will!" His hand clasp is very strong and cold as ice – more like the hand of a dead than living man.'

'Within stood a tall old man, clean-shaven save for a long white moustache, and clad in black from head to foot, without a single speck of colour about him anywhere. . . The old man motioned me in with his right hand with a courtly gesture, saying in excellent English, but with a strange intonation: *"Welcome to my house! Enter freely and of your own will!"* His hand clasp is very strong and as cold as ice – more like the hand of a dead than living man.'

Inside Castle Dracula, it is not as bleak as you might imagine. Far from it – the curtains and furniture are so lavish they remind Harker of Hampton Court.

As he enjoys his meal, Harker studies the Count, 'The mouth, so far as I could see it under the heavy moustache, was fixed and rather cruel-looking, with peculiarly sharp teeth; these protruded over the lips, whose remarkable ruddiness showed astonishing vitality in a man of his years.' When the Count leans over him, he notices the hairs on the palms of his hands and his fingernails cut to sharp points. By now it is nearly dawn, and he shows Harker to his bedroom – 'I have to be away till the afternoon, so sleep well and dream well!' He bows courteously and leaves.

Harker sleeps late after his journey, and finds his breakfast waiting for him after he has dressed. As he explores the rooms he is greatly impressed by all the treasures, though he is surprised there is no servant in sight and not a single mirror anywhere.

When the Count returns they get down to business, and Harker gives him the necessary papers to sign for the house he is buying. As he describes the gloominess of the place – the dark pool, barred windows, derelict chapel and a private lunatic asylum nearby – Count Dracula seems delighted. Again they talk till dawn, when the Count jumps up, excuses himself and leaves.

Next something happens to make Harker feel 'there is something so strange about this place and all in it that I cannot but feel uneasy.'

He has started to shave one morning, using his own small shaving glass, when he is startled to feel a hand on his shoulder and hear the Count say good morning: '. . . it amazed me that I had not seen him, since the reflection of the glass covered the whole room behind me.' Turning to the glass again, he realises there is no reflection – the Count is beside him but cannot be seen in the glass. In his surprise, Harker cuts himself slightly and realises that blood is trickling down his chin – 'I laid down the razor . . . when the Count saw my face, his eyes blazed with a sort of demoniac fury, and he suddenly made a grab at my throat. I drew away, and his hand touched the string of beads which held the crucifix. It made an instant change in him, for the fury passed so quickly that I could hardly believe that it was ever there.'

'Take care,' warns the Count, 'it is more dangerous than you think in this country.' He seizes the glass and throws it out of the window. It shatters into a thousand pieces on the stones of the courtyard far below. The Count leaves, and Harker simply records that 'it is very annoying, for I do not see how I am to shave.' He uses the lid of his watch-case instead. That day, Harker discovers that all the doors in the castle are locked, and he is a prisoner. A night or two later, all of his fears are realised as he looks out of his bedroom window and notices something below:

'What I saw was the Count's head coming out from the window. I did not see the face, but I knew the man by the neck and the movement of his back and arms. In any case, I could not mistake the hands which I had had so many opportunities of studying. I was at first interested and somewhat amused, for it is wonderful how small a matter will interest and amuse a man when he is a prisoner. But my very feelings changed to repulsion and terror when I saw the whole man slowly emerge from the window and begin to crawl down the castle wall over that dreadful abyss, *face down*, with his cloak spreading out around him like great wings.'

When he tries to escape, he enters the cellars

of the castle and finds boxes full of earth in one of the vaults. He raises the lid of one of them:

'I saw something which filled my very soul with horror. There lay the Count, but looking as if his youth had been half-renewed, for the white hair and moustache were changed to dark iron-grey; the cheeks were fuller, and the white skin seemed ruby-red underneath; the mouth was redder than ever, for on the lips were gouts of fresh blood, which trickled from the corners of the mouth and ran over the chin and neck. Even the deep burning eyes seemed set amongst swollen flesh, for the lids and pouches underneath were bloated. It seemed as if the whole awful creature were simply gorged with blood; he lay like a filthy leech, exhausted with repletion.'

He picks up a shovel and brings the edge down on to the Count's face, but the head turns and the eyes fasten on Harker 'with all their blaze of basilisk horror' so that he falters and his blow leaves only a gash on the Count's forehead.

'I saw something which filled my very soul with horror . . . It seemed as if the whole awful creature were simply gorged with blood; he lay like a filthy leech, exhausted with repletion.'

This is a good place to break off and urge you to read the original novel by Bram Stoker for yourself. There is plenty of excitement ahead.

Why did Bram Stoker write *Dracula*? There are several theories. The most popular is that the idea for the story came to Stoker in a dream, in the same way that Mary Shelley's dream gave her the idea for *Frankenstein* – it is believed that Stoker dined too well on dressed crab and had a nightmare.

The Dracula Society claims that Stoker based the Count on the historical Dracula – Vlad the Impaler (see Chapter 8). Certainly he used historical information as background material, and this is how he stumbled on the name. He had the flair to realise what a wonderful title it would make – *Drac-ula* – it echoes as you say it! – the only one of his eighteen books with a single word as the title. But there is no reason to suspect that Vlad was a vampire or even thought of as such.

Many theories have been put forward as to why Bram Stoker wrote *Dracula*, but it could be that the distinguished professors are looking for something that is not there, that in writing *Dracula*, Stoker had a rattling good story to tell and simply wanted to tell it.

Bram Stoker had two sides to his personality. Outwardly he was strong and stalwart, but inwardly he was unsure of himself, and had a particular obsession with the strange and supernatural. He developed this craving when he was a boy, confined to his bed for the first eight years of his life with an illness which has never been explained. To entertain him, his mother Charlotte told him stories of the terrible cholera epidemic that swept across Europe to Western Ireland where she lived with her family when she was a girl. Odd stories for a sickly child, about people buried alive (see Chapter 2) but they made a deep impression on Bram.

After leaving Trinity College, Dublin, Bram followed his father, Abraham, into the Irish Civil Service. To escape from the monotony of his job, he wrote a serial called *The Chain of Destiny*, about a character called 'the phantom of the fiend', for the *Shamrock* magazine, and reviewed plays for the *Dublin Mail* in return for a free seat in the theatre.

Bram Stoker, 1847–1912, the creator of Dracula. *A close friend of the actor, Henry Irving, Bram Stoker gave up his safe career in the Irish Civil Service to partner Irving in running the Lyceum Theatre, London. Right: The Rubrics, Trinity College, Dublin. Bram Stoker studied here as an undergraduate before his fateful meeting with Henry Irving.*

This was how he met the young English actor, Henry Irving. The two became great friends, and when Irving asked Stoker to join him in London a couple of years later, after he had bought the Lyceum Theatre, he did not hesitate. He gave up his safe career in the Civil Service, married Florence Balcombe and sailed for England. His mother commented scornfully, 'He has gone as manager to a strolling player.'

But Stoker's devotion was rewarded. Irving triumphed at the Lyceum and Stoker was able to bask in the actor's reflected glory, meeting all the important 'lions' of the day. All the time he was writing – he wrote eighteen books altogether – and sometimes he managed to holiday on his own, striding across the countryside as if he had a surplus of energy. On a walking tour in Scotland, he stumbled on the small fishing village of Cruden Bay, and it was here that he wrote his masterpiece *Dracula*.

There had been many books on vampires, but Stoker skimmed the cream of all the best vampire legends, and brought them up to date. A Hungarian university professor told him of the superstitions in that part of the world, and the belief that vampires existed in Transylvania across the Hungarian border, and it seems certain that he told Stoker of the real 'Dracula' – a man of extraordinary cruelty (see Chapter 8). With the help of an old guidebook and the library in the British Museum, Stoker's vivid imagination did the rest.

His genius was to place *Dracula* in the setting of contemporary Victorian England. This made the story seem close to home and possible, just as Alfred Hitchcock traps an ordinary man in his films and plunges him into an extraordinary situation. In *Dracula*, Stoker refers to contemporary newspaper reports, Kodak snaps and even an early version of the tape-recorder. Consequently, the fantastic figure of Count Dracula seems more real.

The book was published in 1897. It had a mixed reception, but the most prophetic comment came from his mother Charlotte: 'My dear it is splendid, a thousand miles beyond anything you have written before, and I feel certain will place you very high in the writers of the day. . . No book since Mrs. Shelley's *Frankenstein* or indeed any other at all has come near yours in originality, or terror – Poe is nowhere. I have read much but I have never met a book like it at all. In its terrible excitement it should make a widespread reputation and much money for you.'

This was true of the distant future, but sadly wrong as far as Bram Stoker himself was concerned. *Dracula* has made a fortune for other people in all sorts of ways. It has become an industry of its own, with Dracula kites, Dracula ice lollies, and Dracula fangs that go crunch in the night. Unfortunately, Stoker himself never benefited from all this, and he never enjoyed the fruits of national fame and fortune.

When Henry Irving became the first actor to be honoured with a knighthood, the tide had already started to turn against him. Bad health; a fire that destroyed the warehouse with all the Lyceum's scenery; and the failure of several costly productions led to the loss of his theatre and his death in October 1905. It had been a great friendship and Stoker was desolate. He suffered a slight stroke and from then on had to write with the help of a magnifying glass. His last novel, *The Lair of the White Worm*, is one of the weirdest books ever written and suggests that he was deeply disturbed.

He died in poverty on 20th April, 1912, at the age of sixty-four, and was buried at Golders Green in London. Unhonoured in his lifetime and barely mentioned in encyclopedias, Bram Stoker has been the least-known author of one of the best-known books ever written – until now. At long last he is recognised as a great writer, and the Greater London Council have honoured his memory with a commemorative blue plaque to mark the house where he lived in London.

The Phantom of the Opera

Like most of these horror stories, the original novel by Gaston Leroux published in 1911 is more weird than the familiar film versions.

In his prologue the author claims that this is a true story. It concerns the masked Ghost who is said to haunt the Opera House in Paris. There are numerous cellars and passages in the Opera House – a honeycomb of a place where the phantom can disappear and reappear miraculously, rather like the Hunchback who haunted the ramparts of Notre Dame, but occasionally he is glimpsed as he scurries away. The Ghost's voice is heard everywhere. Eventually it is revealed that in his lifetime he was a brilliant ventriloquist, and his name is Erik. In one of the most dramatic scenes in the novel, Carlotta, the great star of the French opera, appears on stage. The Ghost has threatened that a catastrophe will take place. It does! Suddenly her marvellous voice is transformed into the hideous croak of a toad.

'If I live to be a hundred, I should always hear the super-human cry of grief and rage which he uttered when the terrible sight appeared before my eyes.'

On one level the book is a romance, because the Opera Ghost is in love with Christine Daae, a young, not very talented singer. With his own musical genius, he manages to inspire her, and the first time that the star, Carlotta, falls ill, Christine replaces her and triumphs. Unfortunately, the handsome young Vicomte de Chagny, Raoul, is in love with her too. The Ghost's jealousy is inflamed and finally he traps Christine in his underground lair. Later, she tells Raoul how she confronted the Ghost and unmasked him:

'If I lived to be a hundred, I should always hear the superhuman cry of grief and rage which he uttered when the terrible sight appeared before my eyes . . . imagine, if you can, Red Death's mask suddenly coming to life in order to express, with the four black holes of its eyes, its nose, and its mouth, the extreme anger, the mighty fury of a demon; *and not a ray of light except from the sockets*, for, as I learned later, you cannot see his blazing eyes except in the dark.'

He seizes her hands and digs them into his face, tearing his terrible dead flesh with her nails, and shouting, 'Know that I am built up of death from head to foot and that it is a corpse that loves you and adores you and will never, never leave you! . . . Look, I am not laughing now, I am crying, crying for you Christine, who have torn off my mask and who therefore can never leave me again!'

Gaining his trust, Christine is released by the Ghost on the understanding that she will return, but when he accidentally overhears her plan to escape from Paris with Raoul, he imprisons her again – to live with him forever, or to die.

There is much in the book that does not stand too close an examination. Even though the Ghost wears a pasteboard nose with a moustache attached to it, the ease with which he travels outside the Opera House is never explained. Some parts of the book are silly, but it is the *idea* that is so tremendous. At the end, the Ghost allows the two lovers to leave, realising that Christine can only feel pity for him and not the love and deep affection for which he craves.

Sheridan Le Fanu (1814–73)

Le Fanu has been hailed as 'a master of mystery and horror', and many people have compared him to Poe. He was brilliant in hinting at horror rather than stating it, yet he is still underrated and not as well known as he should be. This is possibly because there is no single masterpiece, like *Dracula*, to make him famous, but several outstanding stories such as *Carmilla* and *Green Tea*. He started writing late in life, when he was nearing fifty, but made up for this by producing twelve books in his last twelve years.

Le Fanu sounds a French name and it came from his Huguenot family which settled in Dublin in the eighteenth century, but he was as Irish as his younger fellow Dubliner, Bram Stoker, on whom he had a profound influence.

His description of the destruction of the female vampire in *Carmilla* was written twenty-five years before *Dracula*, but it lingered in Stoker's imagination:

'The body, therefore, in accordance with the ancient practice, was raised, and a sharp stake driven through the heart of the vampire, who uttered a piercing shriek at the moment, in all respects such as might escape from a living person in the last agony. Then the head was struck off, and a torrent of blood flowed from the severed neck. The body and head were next placed on a pile of wood, and reduced to ashes, which were thrown upon the river and borne away, and that territory has never since been plagued by visits of a vampire.'

'The body, therefore, in accordance with the ancient practice, was raised, and a sharp stake driven through the heart of the vampire, who uttered a piercing shriek at the moment, in all respects such as might escape from a living person in the last agony.'

Green Tea is the story of Mr Jennings – a clergyman haunted by the evil presence of a small black monkey, visible only to himself, even when his eyes are shut. At last it gains too great a control and the clergyman kills himself, leaving a note for the doctor who has been trying to help him:

'Dear Dr Hesselius. – It is here. You had not been an hour gone when it returned. It is speaking. It knows all that has happened. It knows everything – it knows you, and is frantic and atrocious. It reviles. I send you this. It knows every word I have written – I write this. This I promised, and therefore write, but I fear very confused, very incoherently. I am so interrupted, disturbed.'

This is, of course, another tale of conscience (apart from the possible hallucinatory effect of a drug – the 'green tea' – on Mr Jennings). It could be that in the clergyman's past there was something so terrible that he could not endure living with it. With real murderers, guilt often takes the form of anonymous letters accusing themselves of the crime; with Mr Jennings, it was a little black monkey on his back.

Ambrose Bierce, one of the world's masters of the horror story. Ambrose Bierce disappeared without trace in Mexico while covering the Mexican Civil War in 1914.

Ambrose Bierce (1842–1914)

An American journalist and writer of short stories, Bierce is considered one of the masters of horror. When he was a young man he enlisted in the Union Army to fight in the American Civil War, and many of the things he witnessed – such as wild pigs eating the corpses of soldiers – were described in *Tales of Soldiers and Civilians*, published in San Francisco in 1891. His preface revealed that it was published by a friend – 'Denied existence by the chief publishing houses of this country' – but it was more successful in England, his home for four years, where it was called *In the Midst of Life*.

Bierce was a bitter man, and released his venom in a famous newspaper column called *The Prattler*, which he wrote for many years. Another work, his *Devil's Dictionary*, included such sour definitions as this one, for *Handkerchief*: 'a small square of silk or linen used at funerals to conceal lack of tears.'

Bierce's most famous horror stories were published in *Can Such Things Be?* (1893). He resented the lack of recognition he received at the time, but the stories are admired today as classics of horror. He *enjoyed* horror – when he was accused of frightening his readers, he replied, 'If it scares you to read that one imaginary person killed another, why not take up knitting.' The stories include *Moxon's Master*, an early variation on the Frankenstein theme, about a machine which develops powers of thought and runs amok when it loses a game of chess, and *The Death of Halpin Frayser*, which starts with this tremendous paragraph:

'One dark night in midsummer a man waking from a dreamless sleep in a forest lifted his head from the earth, and staring a few moments into the blackness, said: "Catherine Larue." He said nothing more; no reason was known to him why he should have said so much.'

He finds a shallow pool and plunges his hand into it:

'It stained his fingers; it was blood! Blood, he then observed, was about him everywhere. The weeds growing rankly by the roadside, showed it in blots and splashes on their big, broad leaves. Patches of dry dust between the wheelways were pitted and spattered as with a red rain. Defiling the trunks of trees were broad maculations of crimson, and blood dripped like dew from their foliage.'

Bierce had a powerful visual sense, and was proud also of his pure English style. He hated being compared to anyone else, especially Edgar Allan Poe. Poe's tales shriek with humanity – the one quality that Bierce lacks absolutely.

Perhaps the most extraordinary thing about Bierce's private life was his death – he disappeared off the face of the earth when he went to cover the civil war in Mexico. The truth of the end of 'Bitter Bierce', who 'set a level of viciousness and brutality seldom surpassed in American journalism,' will never be known.

Dr M. R. James, 1862–1936.

Dr M. R. James (1862–1936)

Montague Rhodes James knew the power of suggestion of what *might be* rather than what actually *is*. His ghost stories, which are beautifully written, offer no explanations – there is never a neat solution at the end.

Oh, Whistle, and I'll Come to You my Lad is one of James's most celebrated stories and con-

cerns a bronze whistle from another age which, when blown, summons up 'a horrible, an intensely horrible face *of crumpled linen*'.

Considering how delicate James's stories are, they adapt to television surprisingly well. Both *Oh, Whistle, . . .* and *Lost Hearts* have been filmed for the small screen, and the latter came across with special brilliance. A young boy, called Stephen, is staying with his kindly cousin Mr Abney, when he is warned of danger by the ghosts of two children who have been murdered by Mr Abney:

'Whilst the girl stood still, half smiling, with her hands clasped over her heart, the boy, a thin shape, with black hair and ragged clothing, raised his arms in the air with an appearance of menace and of unappeasable hunger and longing. The moon shone upon his almost transparent hands, and Stephen saw that the nails were fearfully long and that the light shone through them. As he stood with his arms thus raised, he disclosed a terrifying spectacle. On the left side of his chest there opened a black and gaping rent; and there fell upon Stephen's brain, rather than upon his ear, the impression of one of those hungry and desolate cries that he had heard resounding over the woods of Aswarby all that evening. In another moment this dreadful pair had moved swiftly and noiselessly over the dry gravel, and he saw them no more.'

Had Stephen imagined this? No. Mr Abney is found dead, his left side torn open in a huge wound, exposing his heart.

In spite of his talent for writing stories full of menace, M. R. James was the least menacing of men: a Professor, former Provost of Eton, a Fellow of All Souls College, Cambridge. He wrote his stories in his spare time, the most famous being *Ghost Stories of an Antiquary*. Did he believe in ghosts? 'I am prepared to consider evidence and accept it if it satisfies me.' This is as far as he was prepared to go. But he did permit himself this warning: 'Be careful how you handle the packet you pick up in the carriage drive, particularly if it contains nailparings and hair. Do not, in any case, bring it into the house; *it may not be alone.*'

Horror on Stage and Screen

'What would a man look like whose brain had been taken from the head of another man, "transplanted as it were"? How would a hand appear that had been "grafted" on to another arm? How would the eyes of a dead man appear if they were suddenly to open?'

(Jack Pierce, make-up man, on his creation of Frankenstein's monster)

Curtains for Dracula

Horror films often develop from stage versions of stories rather than directly from the novels themselves. The best known horror stories were adapted for the stage remarkably early – for instance *Frankenstein* was presented at the Adelphi Theatre, London, in 1850, with the title *Frankenstein, or The Model Man*, and *Jekyll and Hyde* was withdrawn from the Lyceum Theatre in 1888 out of respect to the public, already scared to death by the murders of Jack the Ripper. As for *Dracula*, it is claimed that a stage version is *always* in production somewhere in the world. The birth of *Dracula* on stage, and how this became involved with the cult of the vamp in Hollywood, is a fascinating story.

It starts at ten in the morning on 18th May, 1897, at the great Lyceum Theatre off the Strand in London: 'For the first time – A Drama – in prologue and five acts – DRACULA or the Un-Dead by Bram Stoker.' The cast list revealed that the part of Count Dracula was being taken by a man called Mr Jones – an actor who does not seem to have been heard of before or since.

A few figures huddled inside, including Bram Stoker's cook. What on earth was going on?

The answer is simple. *Dracula* had been published that month and Bram Stoker thought it was possible that his story might be adapted for the stage. But in those days, books were stolen – or 'pirated' – without the author's permission and without payment. The best legal safeguard was the formality of *one* production on stage, complete with poster and programme, which would establish the author's copyright. This was what Stoker was doing, and as he was the Acting Manager of the Lyceum he was able to use his own theatre for the morning read-through. As for 'Admission One Guinea', that was deliberately to *discourage* the public. He did not want them to see it – nor did they.

But a strange process had begun — 1897 was a good year for vampires. Stoker's book had already created an interest which was heightened by a controversial painting called *The Vampire*, shown in the summer exhibition of the New Gallery. Painted by a friend of Stoker's, Philip Burne-Jones, it portrayed a woman leaning over a bare-chested man.

Blood trickled from punctures in his skin. It caused a sensation, and ladies and gentlemen of polite Victorian society flocked to the gallery for a fashionable thrill. The programme accompanying the exhibition contained a poem written by a relative of the painter – Rudyard Kipling. This was also called *The Vampire*, and is a superb read.

'A fool there was and he made his prayer
(Even as you and I!)
To a rag and a bone and a hank of hair
(We called her the woman who did not
    care)
But the fool he called her his lady fair
(Even as you and I).

'The fool was stripped to his foolish hide
(Even as you and I)
Which she might have seen when she
    threw him aside –
(But it isn't on record the lady tried)
So some of him lived but the most of him
    died
(Even as you and I).'

Above and left: Two stills of Theda Bara, the first film star, in Fox's 1917 production of A Fool There Was. *Right:* Nosferatu, *the first Dracula film, 1922.*

With no cinema or television it was possible for a single painting to become a 'celebrity'. *The Vampire* and the accompanying programme crossed the Atlantic and became a sensation in New York where public interest was so keen that a play was presented called *A Fool There Was*. The film rights were bought up by a man called Fox, whose company later became famous as 'Twentieth Century Fox'. He decided to create the first film 'star'. He chose a young actress called Theodosia Goodman, changing her name to Theda Bara, an anagram of *Arab Death*.

Some people say this was a coincidence, but the publicity men seized their chance. The hint of Arabia was perfect for a film about a woman who treated men with contempt. Theda Bara was photographed leaning over a male skeleton, she wore bat-like capes, and it was claimed that she was born in the shade of the pyramids. She gave interviews, in broken English, in darkened hotel bedrooms reeking of incense. It has been said that when the newspapermen left, she would dash across the room, fling back the curtains and open the window with a cry of, 'Gimme some air!'

But the publicity worked. Grateful for a good story, the press played along with the fantasy. Theda Bara was presented to the public as the first 'vamp' in the silent film *A Fool There Was*, which had the sub-title 'Kiss me my fool' – a line that was taken up by young filmgoers. Vamps became the rage. The cult of the vamp or vampire had been established.

Meanwhile, back in England, the stage manager of a provincial repertory company (Jack Howarth, known to millions of British television viewers as Albert Tatlock of *Coronation Street*) loaned his copy of *Dracula* to his producer, Hamilton Deane. Deane, an Irishman like Bram Stoker, was a 'matinee idol' of the English provinces. He sensed the potential success of *Dracula* on stage, bought the rights from Stoker's widow, and adapted it. There was surprisingly little for Dracula to do – the occasional appearance and a few lines, like his curious opening words to the maid: 'I have sorrow if I have given to you the alarm – perhaps my foot-fall sounds not so heavy as that of your English ploughman.' The part went to an actor called Edmund Blake.

Deane was an actor-manager of the old school, with a flair for dramatic effects. His script contained detailed instructions for the actor playing Dracula: 'Trousers must be strapped under feet – one foot to be secured inside window to solid rostrum. The Inverness cape which he wears must be heavily wired, so that when face downwards, it assumes the shape of a bat's wings.' There were tricks with fake coffins full of earth, but as the inventor refused to allow anyone else to use them, he had to be made up as Count Dracula too, with a lot of wig and lifts in his shoes as he was very small! Above all, Deane thought of a brilliant 'gimmick' for his London production in 1927 – a Red Cross nurse in the foyer, just in case someone collapsed from fright. One evening a man was feeling ill and left his seat in the stalls. As he did so, the lights dimmed on stage and he lost his balance, resting his hand on a woman in the row in front of him who was wearing a backless evening dress. She screamed, and both of them *did* faint!

Deane gave himself the best speech in the play, as Van Helsing, and he warns the others of the power of the vampire:

'He is Brute and more than Brute, and the heart of him is not. He cannot die by mere passing of time. So long as he can fatten on the blood of the living – he can grow younger. He can transform himself at will to any of the forms of meaner things: such as the rat – the bat – the wolf. He can come in mist which he creates, or in the moonlight rays as elemental dust. He can vanish at will. He can see in the dark. He can do all these things – yet he is not free. His power ceases, as does that of all evil things, at the coming of day – he can only change himself – at his change time – at Moon, or at exact Sunrise or Sunset.'

But his finest hour came after the curtain had fallen. Deane advanced before the house:

'Just a moment, ladies and gentlemen! Just a word before you leave. We hope the memories of Dracula and Renfield won't give you bad dreams, so just a word of reassurance. When you get home tonight and the lights have been turned out and you are afraid to look behind the curtains and you dread to see a face appear at the window – why, just pull yourself together! And remember that after all THERE ARE SUCH THINGS!'

Bela Lugosi

Bela Lugosi played Dracula on the Broadway stage. He had little need of make-up for he looked sinister already, with strange piercing eyes, and his accent was no problem as he was Hungarian.

Born on 29th October, 1884, his background remains vague. He was either the son of a Baron Lugosi, a banker, or, as some people claim, he took his name from the town where he was born – Lugos – and his first name from the tribe of Bela.

After serving in the Hungarian cavalry, he played small film parts in Europe and then came to Hollywood. Though he appeared in a silent version of *Dr Jekyll and Mr Hyde*, he was not successful as an actor until the English stage version of *Dracula* came to New York and he was given the title role. The play ran for two years and Lugosi's personal triumph made him the obvious replacement for Lon Chaney who died just before the film was started in 1930.

Bela Lugosi had the luck to become the first 'horror star' in the first Hollywood production to be advertised as a 'horror film'. For good measure, the publicity men described it as 'The strangest love a man has ever known.' *Dracula* was an instant success, and this success is entirely due to the hypnotic performance of its star. This is how Lugosi described his approach to his part:

> 'An evil expression in the eyes, a sinister arch to the brow or a leer on my lips – all of which take long practice in muscular control – are sufficient to hypnotise an audience into seeing what I want them to see, and what I myself see in my mind's eye.'

Dracula is the oldest talkie that still plays commercially and, for all its flaws, it is a masterpiece. The effective opening showing Castle Dracula in the Carpathian mountains is surprisingly true to Stoker. The sets may be fake, but they haunt the imagination. Even

Bela Lugosi in the 1931 production of Dracula, *a role which, for so many years, he made his own.*
Inset : The original poster for the 1931 film.

the three vampire women are convincing. Though the attempts at humour are sometimes heavy-handed, there are some good moments, like the dinner party where Count Dracula says, 'I don't drink,' adding *'wine'*, with a sinister smile, as he notices a tempting pin-prick of blood on a guest's hand. When he hears the howling of the wolves, he listens with pleasure and exclaims, 'What music they make!' But Tod Browning, the director, and Lugosi never make the mistake of 'sending up' the story for laughs. They knew that if a vampire is laughed at he is no longer frightening. *Dracula* was safe in their hands and the public enjoyed being horrified.

It was obvious that the film studios should cash in on the horror cult and think of *Frankenstein* as the follow-up. Bela Lugosi now made the greatest mistake of his life. He was the natural choice for the monster, but he was insulted at being offered what he considered an inferior, non-speaking part. He disliked the idea of all that heavy make-up, and wanted his own face to be seen. He turned it down.

The brilliant British director, James Whale, noticed a young actor having lunch in the studio's canteen. He thought he had possibilities and gave him a film test. He got the part. The actor's name was Boris Karloff, who became the new 'horror star'.

Lugosi's health began to deteriorate. As early as 1935 he needed medical attention for 'shooting pains in my legs', and in 1955 he asked to be admitted to hospital for treatment. Though he was a wreck, compared to his vitality when he played Count Dracula in 1931, he started work on another film *The Black Sheep* when he came out of hospital, with the old reliable Lon Chaney Jnr and John Carradine. Lugosi had such difficulty remembering his lines that he was given the part of Casmir, a mute servant. His last role was a scientist in a space film *Plan 9 from Outer Space*. He died on 16th August, 1956, at the age of seventy-two. Lugosi made over a hundred films, but the role of Count Dracula, which earned him £200,000, dominated him right to the end. He was laid to rest in his coffin wearing Dracula's black cloak with its scarlet lining, as he requested, with Dracula's ring on his finger.

Boris Karloff

Hollywood was lucky – or wise – to choose such fine actors for its horror men. Karloff came to the part of Frankenstein's monster after several years' experience. As Peter Underwood relates in his book *Horror Man* (Leslie Frewin 1972), Karloff's real name was William Henry Pratt – no wonder he changed it!

In 1909, at the age of twenty-two, he bought a second-class ticket and sailed to Canada to become a farmer. But the 'acting bug' had bitten him, and he joined a theatrical company for a salary of £6 a week, changing his name from Pratt to Karloff. He was on his way, and

reached Hollywood in 1917. Over the next fourteen years he had a struggle to make ends meet, but learned his craft, appearing in more than fifty silent films, usually as the villain. In 1931 alone he appeared in seventeen films, the climax of which was *Frankenstein*.

'What's the best horror picture you ever made?' Karloff was asked for the rest of his life. The answer was always the same – 'Without a doubt, the original *Frankenstein*.' He added, 'The part was what we call a "natural", any actor who played it was destined for success.' But that was too modest. In spite of his 'horror man' image, Karloff was a kind and gentle man. Lugosi might have portrayed the

monster as something sinister – Karloff made the creature sympathetic. This was his triumph.

If Lon Chaney senior had lived he would have played Count Dracula *and* the monster, and become the greatest horror star in history. Karloff now became the new master of disguise. For three weeks, he spent every evening with the film's make-up man, Jack Pierce, and together they created the monster we think of today. Mary Shelley never described the monster in detail, so they had to start from scratch. Pierce asked himself many questions:

Boris Karloff as he appeared in his last horror film, The Curse of the Crimson Altar, *in 1968.*

'What would a man look like whose brain had been taken from the head of another man, "transplanted" as it were? How would a hand appear that had been "grafted" on to another arm? How would the eyes of a dead man appear if they were suddenly to open? . . . The two metal studs that stuck out of the sides of his neck were inlets for electricity – plugs; not bolts. Don't forget the monster was an electrical gadget and that lightning was his life force . . . Also I had read that the Egyptians used to bind some criminals hand and foot and bury them alive. When their blood turned to water after their death, it flowed into their extremities and stretched their arms to gorilla length and swelled their hands and feet and faces to abnormal proportions. I thought this would make a nice touch for the monster, since he was supposed to be made from the corpses of executed felons. So I fixed Karloff up that way. The lizard eyes were made of rubber, as was his false head. I made his arms look longer by shortening the sleeves of his coat. His legs were stiffened by steel struts and two pair of trousers. His large feet were the boots asphalt-spreaders wear. His finger-nails were blackened with shoe polish . . .'

The result was tremendous, but it was terrible for the actor! When they started filming it took three and a half hours to apply the make-up every morning. Wire clamps pulled down the corners of Karloff's mouth, and the boots weighed eight kilograms each. At the end of the day, it took another one and a half hours to get it all off, and he needed a massage and infra-red treatment to regain the use of his muscles. The metal bolts, or plugs, left two small scars on his neck for some time afterwards. Karloff gave the vital finishing touch by adding his own humanity, which made audiences feel for the monster who wished to be loved and understood. Karloff had no lines to speak but he talked with his eyes. As the producer, Carl Laemmle, put it, 'Karloff's eyes mirrored the suffering we needed.'

For once, Hollywood improved on the original, as far as film effects were concerned: the sight of the monster, the lightning, the brain stolen from a madman – all were new ideas. The result was considered so shocking by the studio that they sneaked the film in a quiet preview in California. When the monster came in backwards, and then turned round and showed his face, half the audience walked out – and then felt they had to go in again! James Whale, the director, was woken by an angry telephone call in the early morning: 'I can't sleep on account of your picture, so I'm darned if you're going to sleep either.'

Frankenstein cost 275,000 dollars to make, but brought in 12 million. Fan-mail began to flow in for Karloff as it had for Lugosi, but with a difference. Many of the letters came from children who felt sorry for the monster. 'The children have never fallen for my nonsense,' said Karloff. 'They sit in the cinema with their eyes glued to the screen. They watch the monster parading his stuff, and now and then give hoots of mock terror or shiver with suppressed excitement, but the moment the word END flashes on the screen, they begin to laugh about Karloff and his antics.'

Karloff went on to play *Fu Manchu*, and a gang leader in the famous gangster film *Scarface*. But a follow-up was inevitable and, in 1935, he appeared in *The Bride of Frankenstein*, also directed by James Whale. This is a sequel to the original film. In it, the scientist creates a female mate for the monster, but when she comes to life she looks at the creature with horror. It is a great moment in a fine film, but Karloff was unhappy that he had to talk this time, 'When the monster did speak I knew that this was eventually going to destroy the character. It did for me anyway.'

He played the monster once more, and stopped. He made 160 films altogether and died in February 1969, having returned to England, at the age of eighty-two. When asked the secret of his energy, he replied, 'Clean living – up to the age of six!'

Boris Karloff in the 1931 version of Frankenstein. *Jack Pierce's make-up took three and a half hours to apply every morning and, with the humanity that Karloff brought to the part, they created the monster that was to become immortal and made* Frankenstein *the greatest horror movie of all time.*
Inset: The original 1931 poster for Frankenstein.

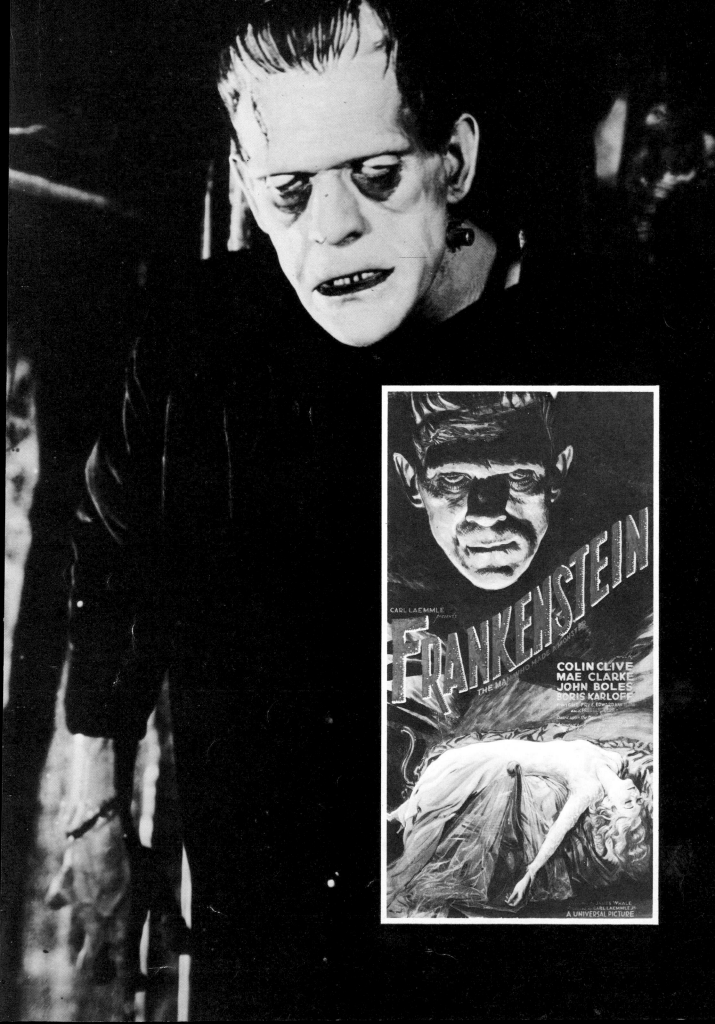

Christopher Lee

By the 1950s it seemed that the horror cult was dead and buried. But, as Jonathan Harker discovered in Castle Dracula, vampires may look dead but they rise again. A year after Lugosi's death the time was ripe for a revival. It took place in England with Hammer Films and a little-known actor called Christopher Lee. For millions of young film-goers, who had never heard the name of Lugosi, Lee became the new Dracula.

Christopher Lee had been acting for ten years, without great success. Tall (1m 96cm), with a commanding personality, dark, and strangely foreign, though he was born in London in 1922, Lee did not fit easily into the role of 'leading man'. In spite of his well-cut tweeds, he was too sinister. But he was perfect for the part of the monster when Hammer decided to remake the great horror films of the 1930s, starting with *The Curse of Frankenstein*: 'I went along and convinced them that I would make a suitable Creature, if only by virtue of my size. I didn't care if they made me totally unrecognisable; I wasn't getting anywhere looking like myself, so I thought that perhaps people would take a little more notice of me if I looked like nothing on earth. The result was the biggest grossing film in the history of the British cinema in relation to cost.'

It was obvious that Hammer Films should follow this success with *Dracula* in 1958, released in America as *Horror of Dracula*. Hammer's horror was something new – in glorious, glossy colour. When blood flowed, you could see it was red. Lee was lucky in having such a fine actor as Peter Cushing as his co-star, playing the role of Mr Right (such as the vampire hunter Van Helsing).

One detail that should not be overlooked was Christopher Lee's *fangs*! Lugosi had never bared his fangs, but Lee plunged his with relish into the white necks of beautiful girls. Then there were such superb effects as the crumbling of Dracula into dust at the end of the film, after Van Helsing has jumped on to the table, making the sign of the crucifix with the giant candlesticks, before pulling down the heavy curtains to let in the light of day.

The cult of Dracula started again. Christopher Lee went on to play him in six more films for Hammer, and became a world star. This is how he explained Dracula's appeal to audiences, when I visited him at his home in London's Cadogan Square:

'He has a strange dark heroism. He offers the illusion of immortality, the subconscious wish we all have for limitless power . . . a man of tremendous brain and physical strength . . . he is either a reincarnation or he has never died. In many ways, he is everything people would like to be – the anti-hero, the heroic villain.'

He spoke as if he had met him!

But Lee began to be trapped in the part, just like Lugosi who was forced to appear in such parodies as *Old Mother Riley meets the Vampire*, in 1952. As an admirer of Bram Stoker's original novel, Lee looks back on that first production with particular pleasure:

'That was the first time I had played Dracula and in that film he did resemble Bram Stoker's creation in many ways, except in appearance, which was wrong and remained wrong in every subsequent film version of the story. The Dracula of the book wore a coat, while all this business of cloaks and opera capes comes from the old Universal pictures.'

So it is easy to understand Lee's indignation as Dracula moved even further from Transylvania and was cast in such unlikely settings as swinging London, in *Dracula A.D. 1972*.

It cannot have been easy, but Christopher Lee at last managed to break free from Count Dracula, with whom he had become identified. He even resigned from the Presidency of the Dracula Society, explaining, 'I am no longer associated with the screen portrayal of the character.' He has proved his versatility as an actor with his success as Mycroft Holmes, Sherlock's brother, and more recently as a James Bond villain. Today he lives in Hollywood, but like it or not (and he does not), for millions of people Christopher Lee *is* Dracula.

Hammer Films brought new life to horror movies in the 1950s and the 1960s. As a result, Christopher Lee became Count Dracula for a new generation. Here he is in the 1970 production, The Scars of Dracula.

Almost Human

*'He's afraid of the witch doctor,
he lives in terror of the evil spirits,
he is afraid of the dark . . .
he lives in continual horror of offending
the leopard men.'*

Negley Farson

The Leopard Men

Leopard men sound colourful, but the things they did were horrible. It helps to understand them if you remember that Africa has witnessed some of the first and fiercest clashes between man and animal. It is not surprising that primeval instincts have lingered on for centuries in regions which have remained primitive for so long. Hunter and hunted – the two were inseparable, almost interchangeable. The Bushmen of South Africa used to give their children the hearts of leopards to eat, to make them brave. If the heart could achieve this, imagine the power of the soul.

One hundred years ago it was commonly believed in West Africa that if a witch doctor and a dangerous animal such as a leopard became blood brothers, the witch doctor would gain power and the animal would become his 'familiar' or slave and kill his enemies for him. This special relationship would last until the death of either party.

Such beliefs were widespread along the coasts of Guinea and Sierra Leone, down to Benin, Nigeria, and the Zaire basin. Leopard Societies flourished in these regions, not always in secrecy. In 1895, a *Human Leopard Society Ordinance* was passed in Sierra Leone, punishing anyone who possessed a leopard skin or the three-pronged weapon that imitated a leopard's claws. During the next seven years a court sentenced eighty-seven men to death for leopard murders. These men believed they shared the strength of a leopard once they wore his skin, in the same way as the *berserkirs*, ancient Norse warriors of Scandinavian legend, believed that they inherited the strength of bears when they wore their skins in battle.

In 1939, the American writer Negley Farson (the author's father) made a journey across Africa, which he recorded in his book *Behind God's Back*. He found evidence that the leopard men still existed in the twentieth century and wrote:

'It is a fact that the Society of the Leopard still carries on, is even thought to be growing, in these parts; of men with steel claws who kill women. . . This Society of the Leopards is so secret, so powerful, that even the native police are too terrified to inform on them. They are, as the Governor said, an almost insoluble African mystery . . . the African *lives all his life in a constant state of dread.* He's afraid of the witch doctor, he lives in terror of the evil spirits, he is afraid of the dark, the things that are in it, he lives in continual horror of offending the leopard men.'

The leopard men took advantage of this 'horror' in the Mau Mau troubles, which resulted in the arrest of Jomo Kenyatta in 1952, though he became President later. One of the 'terrorists' was Dedan Kimathi, who wore a leopard skin and leopard hood for his attacks until he was captured.

Undoubtedly, part of the power of the leopard men came from the belief that when they dressed as leopards they *were* leopards, possessing the strength of the animal and inspired by his spirit.

The Island of Dr Moreau

H. G. Wells was a brilliant writer with a vivid imagination, shown in such books as *The Invisible Man* and *The War of the Worlds*. In *The Island of Dr Moreau* he touches on a universal theme – the attempt to make a man live longer by injecting him with parts of animals. But Wells's fictional Dr Moreau did it the other way round – he tried to change animals into men, with hideous results.

The story, set in 1887, is told as though it were true. A shipwrecked man is picked up by a passing vessel, bound for Hawaii. Two passengers are to be dropped off on a remote island, and the narrator notices that one man looks peculiar – he is misshapen, short, broad and clumsy, with a crooked back, a hairy neck and a head sunk between his shoulders. The dogs on board howl whenever he comes near them.

Montgomery, the other man, persuades the narrator to leave the ship with them. Arriving at the island, he finds it inhabited by 'beast men'. He believes they have once been animals, but now they are even able to talk. These creatures are the results of Dr Moreau's experiments, and the horror of the book lies in the agony the animals have to suffer.

Asked why he has chosen the human form as his model, the doctor replies: 'I suppose there is something in the human form that appeals to the artistic turn of mind more powerfully than any animal shape can.'

When he is accused of cruelty, he defends himself by claiming that 'The study of Nature makes a man at least as remorseless as Nature.' He created monsters almost for the fun of it and has also made a leopard man, a satyr-like creature both ape and goat and several creatures similar to wolves.

The narrator gradually realises that the experiments are not the worst of Moreau's cruelty:

'Before they had been beasts, their instincts fitly adapted to their surroundings, and happy as living things can be. Now they stumbled in the shackles of humanity, lived in a fear that never died, fretted by a law they could not understand; their mock human existence began in an agony, was one long internal struggle, one long dread of Moreau – and for what? It was the wantonness that stirred me.'

The creatures begin to change back into animals, and take their revenge on Moreau. The narrator escapes and returns to civilisation, but finds it hard to adapt to mankind after beasts, for 'I could not persuade myself that the men and women I met were not also another, still passably human, beast people, animals half-wrought into the outward image of human souls . . .'

This is a nightmare of a book, and anyone who respects animals will find it especially odious. Dr Moreau was possessed by a monstrous idea, in every sense, but are we all that much better? We eat animals, hunt them, cage them and make them perform tricks for us in circuses. I believe that the experiments for which animals are used in the name of vivisection and medical research are even worse, and worst of all is the use of animals to test cosmetics – to make *us* look prettier and feel better. White rabbits have shampoo inserted in their eyes for 'irritation' tests, beagles are forced to smoke to test the effects of tobacco fumes and monkeys are subjected to intense noise and reared in isolation with parts of their brains removed. Can anything be more horrible than that?

Every week 100,000 animals die in British laboratories. This makes Dr Moreau look like an amateur, in spite of today's explanation that these deaths are 'in a good cause'.

And what about the dolphin, that wise and affectionate creature whose natural home is in the depths of the sea? He is often kept in a side-show in a tub little bigger than a large bath, with people staring and music blaring. *That* is true horror.

H. G. Wells, 1866–1946. Born in London, H. G. Wells was apprenticed as a young man to a draper. Quickly abandoning this career, he had a short spell of teaching before becoming a journalist and author. Today, he is best remembered for the way in which so many of his predictions in such books as War of the Worlds *and* The Shape of Things to Come *are now reality.*

The Island of Dr Moreau *is an horrific book. Anyone who respects animals will find it a nightmare. But have we improved today? We make animals perform tricks for our amusement and allow animals to suffer cosmetic testing experiments – just to make women look prettier.*

Wolf children

The story of the Wolf children of Midnapore is the most interesting and best documented of all such cases. It happened in India, in this century. The inhabitants of a village in Bengal were so frightened by a 'man ghost' they had seen on the outskirts that they asked for the help of the Reverend J. A. L. Singh, missionary to the local orphanage. They hoped he might be able to perform an exorcism.

After building a tree platform in the jungle, near the place where the 'man ghost' had been seen, the Reverend Singh and his companions climbed on top and waited patiently for an hour. He recorded the event that followed in his diary:

'October 9 1920: All of a sudden, a grown wolf came out from one of the holes, which was very smooth on account of their constant egress and ingress. This animal was followed by another of the same size and kind. The second was followed by a third, closely followed by two cubs one after the other. The holes did not permit two of them together.

'Close after the cubs came the "ghost" – a hideous looking being – hand, feet and body like a human being; but the head was a big ball of some thing covering the shoulders and the upper portions of the bust, leaving only a sharp contour of the face visible, and it was human. Close at its heels there came another awful creature like the first, but smaller in size. Their eyes were bright and piercing, unlike human eyes.

'The first ghost appeared on the ground up to its bust, and placing its elbows on the edge of the hole looked at this side and that side, and jumped out. It looked all round the place from the mouth of the hole before it leaped out to follow the cubs. It was followed by another tiny ghost of the same kind, behaving in the same manner. Both of them ran on all fours.

'My friends at once levelled their guns to shoot at the ghosts. They would have killed them if they had not been dissuaded by me. I held their barrels and presented the field glasses . . . and told them I was sure that these ghosts were human children.'

The missionary had to go to another village where the men knew nothing of the ghosts to hire workers who started to dig out the wolves' lair a week later, with instructions not to shoot. While they were at work one wolf appeared and raced into the jungle, then the second, equally frightened, but the third, the mother wolf, flew at the men in rage, howling, gnashing its teeth, fiercely defending the hole and her young inside it.

Singh watched with admiration. He was amazed at the strength of the mother's feelings for creatures which she had probably originally brought in as food for her cubs.

Meanwhile, the others pierced the wolf with arrows and she fell dead. Then the door was dug out and they entered the cave. The two cubs and the two 'ghosts' were huddled together snarling in one corner.

Sending for several big sheets, the men succeeded in separating them. The cubs were given to the villagers and the other two – the ghosts – were brought to the house of a frightened villager. Curiously, the missionary did not return for several days. When he did, he found that the children had been left without food or water and were in a terrible state. He sprinkled water on their faces and gave them some to drink, and then carried them home.

For the head of an orphanage, Singh was surprisingly stupid. He had forced the children into another terrible transition. They had changed course already, from the weaning by human milk to wolf milk; they ran swiftly on all fours to keep pace with the cubs; their eyes had grown used to the dark; their sense of smell was highly developed. Remarkable though this was, they had no choice. They had to behave like wolves or die. Now they did not know what to do or, indeed, what they were.

Feeding was a problem which he solved at first by tearing up his handkerchief and rolling it into a wick. He dipped one end into a cupful of tea and the other into the child's mouth, and in this way got them to drink. But the change back to human life was not easy. The children's health grew worse and their bodies became covered with deep sores. Then they seemed to recover and grew stronger on a diet of raw milk and raw meat.

Singh, who was not imaginative, named the girls Kamala and Amala. He guessed they were aged eight and eighteen months. He does not seem to have known, however, if they had been abandoned or stolen by the wolf from the cornfields.

Soon they were crawling, not upright but not entirely on all fours as before. In their lair it would have been difficult to stand up even if they had wanted to, but now they had freedom of movement. They were accepted by the other children in the orphanage as neglected

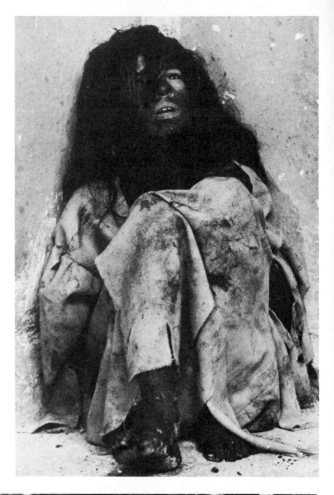

Stills from François Truffaut's 1969 film, L'Enfant Sauvage (The Wild Child). *This film is a beautiful essay on teaching, and the giving, and eventual receiving of love. The 'wild child' is a baby abandoned in the woods of France and discovered years later around 1797.*

106

children who were particularly weak. They took a liking to a year-old baby who was just starting to walk, but one day, discovering that he was different, they turned on him savagely and he never went near them again. All the time they made no sound, apart from howling at night.

The missionary was fascinated by the ease with which the children's limbs had become like those of animals, to make their movements easier, when they had only the wolves to copy. To do him justice he tried to avoid the sensational publicity that began to focus on Midnapore as the story of the children spread by word of mouth. Mrs Singh was a kindly, calm woman who spent hours massaging the children's limbs, as they learnt new movements. From lapping their food like dogs, they took it by hand. Their eyes grew accustomed to the light, so that day and night became separate. The mother wolf had not been able to give them a sense of humour, but she had not taught them anything evil. They knew no malice, no cowardice, no jealousy. Though she was unable to laugh, Kamala cried when her companion Amala died on 21st September, 1921.

Kamala stood upright for the first time two years later, though she continued to run on all fours. Her natural distrust of humans gradually disappeared. She wore clothes, she no longer ate raw meat, and by 1927 she could make herself understood. By then only the bumps on her knees and elbows, her flared nostrils and her bent shape made her different from the other children at the orphanage, who were extremely fond of her. Even so, her intelligence was like that of a three-year old, and her speech was limited to thirty words when she was sixteen. She died on 4th November, 1939. The doctor's certificate stated that, 'Kamala, commonly known as the Wolf Girl, a girl of the Reverend Singh's orphanage, expired this morning at 4 a.m.'

It is possible to conclude from this strange story that human children can adapt to animal life with surprising ease. This seems to be a logical explanation for the mythical werewolf.

A Geographical Guide to Horror

*'The eyes were the worst.
It was not my imagination. They
were in truth like the eyes of a dead
man, not blind but staring
unfocused, unseeing.'*

(The Magic Island *by* William Seabrook)

Haiti – home of the Zombie

Across the Atlantic from West Africa, where the Leopard Men practised witchcraft, lies the island of Voodoo – Haiti.

African slaves were sent there when it was a French colony by King Louis XIII. He gave slave-rights to his colonists, and they tried to convert the Africans to the Catholic Church.

Most of the West African slaves came from the Congo, now known as Zaire. Transported to a strange island, they brought their superstitions with them, and worshipped the ancestors they left behind in the African forests. In Haiti their primitive religion became Voodoo. It was banned to begin with, but forced into secrecy it became even stronger and more sinister. It was an explosive situation, for their French masters treated them abominably, cutting off their hands for trivial offences.

The first slaves arrived in the mid-seventeenth century. Selling them was big business, and a hundred years later as many as 30,000 slaves were landed in Haiti every year. As one generation replaced another, a terrible yearning set in for the past, and the first revolutionary attempt at African independence took place in Haiti in 1757, led by Macandal, a slave from Guinea. Escaping from his plantation, he led a rebellion of fanatical fugitives, but he was captured and burnt to death. Several revolts followed until Jean Jacques Dessalines (1758–1806) proclaimed Haitian independence in 1804.

As Catholicism departed with the French colonists, Voodoo was established as the new religion. Voodoo was thrilling. It celebrated the past with the rhythmic beat of African drums, driving the dancers into such a state of frenzy that they collapsed – a sort of mass hysteria. Blood was essential for ceremonies – usually the sacrifice of such animals as pigs or hens, but occasionally of the 'hornless goat' or human being. There was a famous case in 1863 when a small girl was strangled at a New Year's ceremony, then cut up, and her flesh eaten along with other ritual foods. The next year eight Haitians were publicly executed for eating another girl. Such stories of cannibalism are rare, but they gave Haiti a bad name.

Voodoo ceremonies took place in *tonnelles* – rough huts with mud floors in a back street out of town. They were conducted by Houngans, priests who practised both Wanga (black magic) and bush medicine, either with the medicinal use of leaves or with the use of

108

poison. The Houngans were able to summon up spirit gods, and these could take possession of the dancers. When the spirit god was the ancient Papa Legba, the dancer became old and lame and the others would run forward with sticks and crutches to help him. The African god Agassa, half-panther, half-woman, made the possessed dancers stiffen their fingers into claws. Evil spirits threw the dancers into convulsions. Possession could last several hours and was sometimes so strong that the Haitians could walk on burning coals or hold their hands in boiling water without flinching. It was this atmosphere that created the Zombie, the living dead of the West Indies.

All Haitians were brought up to believe in stories of werewolves and black magic. They were probably the most superstitious people on earth. They believed that a sorcerer could

dig up a grave before the body had time to rot, and lead the corpse away to become his servant. This was a Zombie. The peasants took every possible precaution against this, such as sewing up the corpse's mouth or filling it with earth, to stop it answering if the sorcerer called; they also piled stones on top of the grave and guarded it carefully until the body had rotted.

How do you recognise a Zombie? By his glassy-eyed stare and nasal twang. He is obedient until he is given salt – this releases

William Seabrook, 1886–1945, American author and expert on Voodoo.

him, and is the basis of the most interesting case-history about Zombies, recorded by William Seabrook, an American writer and expert on the subject. In 1918, peasants were needed for work in the canefields. Conscripted in various ways, they poured into the area. One old headman, known as Colombier, led a band of ragged, shuffling creatures. They seemed dazed by their new surroundings and frightened by the noise and smoke of the factories, but became more subdued when they reached the canefields and started to work.

Colombier's wife, Croyance, felt sorry for the Zombies, especially in the evening when they sat around dumbly, eating the tasteless food that was their compulsory diet, without any enjoyment. After several months there was a local fête, and as Colombier was away she acted on a sudden impulse and led the Zombies there as a treat. But they sat down in their usual stupor, seeing nothing.

111

Croyance now made her fatal mistake. She bought some biscuits to cheer them up, but unknown to her they were made from ground, *salted* peanuts. As they nibbled their biscuits, all their senses returned and they gave a cry of anguish, knowing they were dead.

They walked into the sunlight, a grim procession as they stumbled back to their native village. As they entered it, they were recognised by relatives and friends, who quickly spread the news of their return. Wives, children, fathers and mothers wept with happiness as they saw them, but the Zombies shuffled on sightlessly. A mother screamed and fell at her daughter's feet, but the girl walked over her.

When they reached their former graves, the Zombies began to claw at the stones. The moment they touched the earth of their former resting place they collapsed and, within a moment, were little more than rotting flesh. Their families buried them for the second time, then lay in ambush for Colombier and cut off his head when he passed.

Unlike the vampire or the werewolf, it is likely that some creature called the Zombie does – or did – exist. Certainly the Haitians believed in Zombies themselves, but more than 95 per cent of them remain in a primitive state of ignorance to the present day. If they believed that 'fire-hags' could hang up their skins at home and set fire to the canefields, if they believed in the vampire who sucked the blood of children and whose hair turned red in consequence, or in the werewolf that took the form of a dog, killing lambs and sometimes babies, then it is hardly surprising that they believed in Zombies too.

'They walked into the sunlight, a grim procession as they stumbled back to their native village. As they entered it, they were recognised by relatives and friends, who quickly spread the news of their return.'

112

The question remains: what really is a Zombie? William Seabrook helps to answer with this description of a Zombie he met, 'The eyes were the worst. It was not my imagination. They were in truth like the eyes of a dead man, not blind but staring unfocused, unseeing.' He remembered the face of a dog he had seen in a laboratory in Columbia. The entire front brain of the animal had been removed in an operation, and although it was still alive, its eyes were like that of a Zombie. He spoke, but there was no response. Suddenly he was certain that Zombies were nothing more than 'poor ordinary demented human beings, idiots forced to toil in the fields.'

But the most convincing definition of a Zombie is the official statement, Article 246 in the old Penal Code of Haiti, which explains the transformation of a man into a Zombie:

'Also to be termed intention to kill, by poisoning, is *the use of substances* whereby a person is not killed but reduced to *a state of lethargy*, more or less prolonged, and this without regard to the manner in which the substance were used or what were their late result. If following the state of lethargy the person is buried, then the attempt will be termed murder.'

What substances? Obviously the skilful use of drugs, probably made from local plants which we know nothing about.

A Voodoo trance could last for several days, in which the Zombie went about his work hardly realising it. Obviously it was very useful for the boss to have such a willing, uncomplaining slave. This was the motive for supplying the Zombie with drugs. He could move, eat, hear and even speak, but had no memory of his past or knowledge of his present, hideous condition. He was little more than a beast of burden brought by drugs to a state almost indistinguishable from death.

In Haiti today, Voodoo has been reduced to a tourist attraction for the entertainment of foreigners. But this means it is still practised. Who knows what undercurrents linger beneath the jolly surface of tourism . . .?

The Place of Dread

This is the northern tip of Makin-Meang, the northernmost island of the Gilberts in the Central Pacific. It is described in Arthur Grimble's excellent study of primitive life – *A Pattern of Islands* (1952).

Grimble heard weird stories about the ghosts of Makin-Meang before he went there as District Officer. Makin-Meang was regarded by the Gilbertese as a halfway stop between the living and the dead. Anyone who died on the Gilberts had to go to the north of this island, if they wanted to continue to paradise, and had to pass Nakaa, the Watcher at the Gate.

If he died on one of the other fifteen Gilbert Islands, he took the western path to the north of Makin-Meang, but the ghosts of local people took the eastern side. Either route was all right for the living islanders when they travelled north, for they were going *with* the stream of ghosts, provided they never, ever looked back. The danger lay in the return journey. Then it was vital to take the emptier, eastern route, and find out beforehand if anyone had died that day. If you met a ghost face-to-face, you had no hope.

Grimble asked the Native Magistrate to find him a guide who would take him to the Place of Dread. The Magistrate yielded, against his will, supplying him with a giant of a man, a local constable, who would act as guide. This man warned Grimble not to look back as they took the road north, because if he did so, and saw a ghost, he would die within the year.

 So they set off, carrying a large seed-coconut as a gift to plant in Nakaa's grove. Grimble, as a stranger on his first visit, had to carry it, and suspected that the constable had deliberately picked a heavy one. They reached the Place of Dread, which was 'merely a blazing acre or two of coral rock,' and planted the coconut.

By now Grimble was desperately thirsty and asked his guide for a drink of coconut milk. The man was horrified – he said the trees belonged to Nakaa and could not be touched.

So they started the dry journey back, along the eastern coast, with the constable keeping a sullen forty paces behind. Grimble's thirst was so bad that he made up his mind to ignore the guide and ask anyone he met, anywhere, to

Insets below and right: Arthur Grimble. His excellent book, A Pattern of Islands, *describes what life was like for a young administrator in the Colonial Office who was sent out to the western Pacific in 1913.*

pick him a nut from the top of a tree. And then, across the curving beach ahead, he saw a figure coming towards him. 'My eyes never left him, because my intent was pinned on his getting me that drink.' The man drew closer. He walked with a limp, and was a grizzled man of fifty or so, dressed rather ceremoniously. As he came up, Grimble noticed that his left cheek was scarred from the jawbone to the temple.

But did the man see him? To Grimble's astonishment he passed by and continued on his journey as if Grimble did not exist. 'I was shocked speechless. It was so grossly unlike the infallible courtesy of the islanders.'

Then he thought the man might be a lunatic. He called out to the constable to stop him, so he could find out who he was. But the constable did not seem to hear, probably because of the sound of the surf, and ignored the man as he passed by.

Grimble ran back to him. 'Who is that man?' he asked. The constable stopped, bewildered. Then, as Grimble repeated his question, sweat broke out on his forehead. 'I am afraid in this place!' he screamed, high in his head, like a woman, and, without another word, he bolted out on the beach with an arm guarding his eyes.

When Grimble arrived at the house of the Native Magistrate, he found the constable on the verandah. Grimble told the Magistrate what had happened and described the stranger who had passed by so rudely. He mentioned the limp and the scar. The Native Magistrate exchanged nods with the constable. 'That was indeed Na Biria,' he murmured. Grimble asked to see the man, only to be told, 'He is dead. He died this afternoon, soon before three o'clock.'

Grimble stood there dumbfounded. Suddenly he saw Na Biria, at the moment of death, projecting his dying thought, with sixty generations of fear behind it, along that eastern road to the Place of Dread. 'Had I received the impact of his thought as it passed my way? Or if not, what was it I had seen?'

If the man had died at three, he would not yet be buried. Grimble demanded to see his body. The constable was frightened by the idea, but the Magistrate was a Christian (who should know better than to believe in such things) and told Grimble to follow him. They heard the mourners a hundred metres away. They were beating the walls of their houses with sticks, to frighten away strange ghosts. Seeing them so earnestly at work, Grimble recovered his sense of decency. 'These folk believed utterly in what they were doing. For them, the dead man's whole eternity depended on their ritual. For them, the intrusion of me, a stranger, would send him to certain strangulation in Nakaa's net.' He turned away and the Native Magistrate followed him in silence.

Of course Grimble was right, but the questions he leaves behind are tantalising – would he have recognised the corpse? Would he have had a scar on his left cheek? Was he the limping man on the beach?

If so, he would have had certain proof of thought transference at the moment of death.

117

Whitby

If you go to Whitby on the Yorkshire coast of England, take a copy of Bram Stoker's *Dracula* with you. Few towns in England have changed so little since the 1890s when Stoker stayed here.

Whitby lies in a valley, cut in half by the River Esk, and part of its charm lies in the fishing boats that are still busy in the harbour. Walk across the bridge that links the two sides of the town, past a cluster of fine old houses, and up the 199 stone steps known as the Church Stairs to St Mary's Church with the ruined Abbey behind. After such a climb, you may be glad to sit on one of the wooden benches in the graveyard. If you find the place in *Dracula*, you will find it exactly as Stoker described it, give or take a few cars and the sound of the fun fair drifting across the river. The magnificent sepia prints by the great Victorian photographer Sutcliffe (1853–1941), exhibited in the town, confirm how little has changed.

The graveyard is extraordinary. Most of the tombstones have kept their shape, though salt winds have worn away the lettering and darkened the stone. They stand in high wild grass like black lines of surf. There is an appropriate atmosphere of neglect, which appealed to Bram Stoker. 'This is, to my mind, the nicest spot in Whitby, for it lies right over the town, and has a full view of the harbour and the bay to where the headland called Kettleness stretches into the sea.' This is from 'Mina Murray's Journal', but plainly echoes Stoker's own feelings. 'There are walks with seats beside them, through the churchyard; and people go and sit there all day long . . .'

This is the place where Dracula came to England, when his ship with the huge boxes of earth and the dead captain lashed to the wheel was hurled ashore in a terrible storm. There was no sign of life aboard except for a great dog that leapt on to the sands and bounded up the cliff towards the graveyard. This was Dracula!

You can see the elegant curve of East Crescent from the wooden benches, and it was from her window there that Mina Murray (Jonathan Harker's fiancée) looked out in the evening in the hope of seeing her friend Lucy in her favourite seat, after Lucy had disappeared.

'Then as the cloud passed I could see the ruins of the Abbey coming into view; and as the edge of a narrow band of light as sharp as a sword-cut moved along, the church and the churchyard became gradually visible. Whatsoever my expectation was, it was not disappointed, for there on our favourite seat, the silver light of the moon struck a half-reclining figure, snowy white. The coming of the cloud was too quick for me to see much, for shadow shut down on light almost immediately; but it seemed to me as though something dark stood behind the seat where the white figure shone, and bent over it. What was it, whether man or beast, I could not tell.'

Mina hurries across the valley, down the narrow streets and up the steep steps:

'My knees trembled and my breath became laboured as I toiled up the endless steps to the Abbey. I must have gone fast, and yet it seemed to me as if my feet were

The beautiful fishing port of Whitby is the unlikely setting for part of the Dracula story. Photographed by the great Frank Sutcliffe at the turn of the century, it is little changed today.

weighted with lead and as though every joint in my body was rusty. When I got almost to the top I could see the seat and the white figure. I called in fright – "Lucy! Lucy!" – and something raised a head and from where I was I could see a white face and red gleaming eyes . . .'

Mina barefoot and Lucy in her night-dress, they scurry down the steps and through the back lanes to the safety of the Crescent. But Dracula's fangs have claimed their first victim in Britain and poor Lucy is doomed.

Transylvania

Yes, there is such a place! It is not a fantasy land dreamt up by a film company, like Ruritania, but a state in northern Romania near the borders of Hungary. It is much as Stoker described it in *Dracula* in 1897, and this is remarkable, because he never set foot there himself. He gained his research from a Baedeker's guide, books in the British Museum, and information from his Hungarian friend, Professor Arminius Vambery.

It is strange to stand today in Bistrita – called Bistritz in the novel – where Jonathan Harker stayed the night before he left for Castle Dracula. Unlike many of Romania's cities, which are extremely modern, Bistrita is pleasantly old-fashioned. There is a delightful restaurant with a local orchestra, rich in atmosphere, and a small wooden hotel that could have been the model for Stoker's 'Golden Krone'; for good measure there is a coffinmaker's opposite. Now a big modern hotel has been completed, named 'The Golden Crown' to please Dracula-minded visitors!

These photographs were taken in Transylvania, a state in the north of Romania, by members of the Dracula Society. Given the atmosphere, it is easy to see how the Dracula legend has grown up in this area.

Leaving Bistrita, you enter the Borgo Pass. It is splendid, rolling countryside. No wonder Jonathan Harker lost his 'ghostly fears in the beauty of the scene' as he drove through it. He referred to 'a green sloping land full of forests and woods, with here and there steep hills, crowned with clumps of trees or with farmhouses . . .' It is all there still – the huts with wood-shingled roofs, orchards of plums, solitary stone crosses by the roadside, and the occasional figure of a shepherd – when you can see them all in the white mists that swirl around.

One thing is missing – Castle Dracula. It belonged to Stoker's imagination alone, and that is the problem. Ever since one of the major world airlines started 'A Tour Package with a Toothy Grin – an eighteen day fully escorted romp through middle Europe called "Spotlight on Dracula"', Dracula Tours have flown in from all over the world. Tourists expect to see Castle Dracula and the places Stoker wrote about, but they are shown the wrong Dracula instead! British tourists on the recent 'Dracula Tours' arranged by a British airline company have seen fascinating parts of Southern Romania but they haven't gone near Transylvania. Instead they have been shown the fortresses and churches associated with the historical Dracula, Vlad the Impaler (see Chapter 8).

Below: The Romanian national hero, Vlad the Impaler, often seen as the prototype for Count Dracula, lived in this house for four years.

Vlad the Impaler is said to have executed hundreds of people in front of this church in southern Romania.

This has placed the Romanian government in a dilemma. To begin with they did not want their national hero, Vlad, labelled as a ghoul and vampire. Stoker's novel has never been translated into Romanian, and at first they could not understand what all the fuss was about. Gradually they realised they had a tourist gold-mine on their back doorstep. Consequently, they are proposing to direct the Dracula tours to the north, and build a Castle Dracula especially. They are thinking big. With tapes of wolves howling along the Borgo Pass, a calèche with four coal-black horses to take passengers on their final stage of the fearful journey, bats on wires and waitresses with fangs serving the appropriate food and drink (red wine, of course), it could be a triumph – a horror version of Disneyland.

Meanwhile, the only visitors who see the Dracula-landscape of Stoker's novel are independent travellers or those who have joined the Dracula Society on their recent tours in which they covered 1,600 kilometres in twelve days. Bernard Davies, the Honorary Secretary, wrote:

'The trip was simply magnificent. I don't know what the others were expecting, but the journey came up to my expectations all the way. The Romanians pulled out all the stops to give us a good time and really entered into the spirit of the thing The hospitality was terrific, especially the Jonathan Harker luncheon at Bistrita ('roast beef of outlaws' and 'butcher's meat with pepper' on the menu), which developed into the most gigantic binge lasting (I think) until about two in the morning. What a day! . . . Beautiful cloudless weather either end; just two days in the middle round the Borgo Pass appropriately dark and stormy, and when we picnicked up in the Calimani Mountains round a big fire . . . it actually snowed on us. We even managed to have a fight with a band of gypsies! It simply was the most amazing experience. How Bram Stoker would have envied us!'

Highgate cemetery, London

A wonderfully eerie spot, even on a bright sunny morning. The cemetery is divided into two parts and though most people flock to the lower half to see the massive monument to Karl Marx, the north is more mysterious.

Highgate cemetery was designed by the foremost Victorian architects and landscape gardeners, with arches and steps and graceful avenues for the mourning families to walk through. It contains 100,000 tombs, so it is full now. It was a noble concept, but the northern part is so overgrown that foxes prowl through the woods at night and more than twenty varieties of birds live in the undergrowth. This makes it sound romantic, and it is, except that many of the graves have been broken into and tombstones overturned as if a legion of vampires has risen up and heaved them aside.

In fact, people have claimed that they saw a huge vampire hovering over the graves. One hundred vampire hunters invaded the cemetery on 13th March, 1970, and vandalised the tombs. One unfortunate man, who parked his car nearby, returned in the morning to find his car broken into and a headless body propped up against the steering wheel!

The leading vampire hunter, and self-styled High Priest of the Occult Society, was jailed in 1974. He was charged with entering catacombs in consecrated ground ('Capers among the Catacombs' as one newspaper described it) and offering indignity to the remains of a body 'to the great scandal and disgrace of religion, decency and morality.' Police found salt scattered around his room at home and a wooden cross under his pillow, and claimed that voodoo dolls with pins in them had been posted to possible police witnesses against him. He was released in the summer of 1976, claiming that he had held witchcraft ceremonies inside the jail ('there was a flourishing coven when I left'). At least he vowed never to stalk Highgate again. This is just as well, for the place needs all the help it can receive in the struggle against weeds, neglect and such publicity. It was closed temporarily in April 1975, but a Society called 'The Friends of Highgate' are now doing their best to restore it to a more reasonable condition.

Real Horrors

*'My knife is nice and sharp I
want to get to work right away if I
get a chance. Good Luck.
Yours truly,
Jack the Ripper'*

(Letter to a newspaper, 1888)

The Countess Bathory

She was possibly the cruellest woman ever to have lived. No one is sure how many women she killed, but estimates hover around six hundred. Born in 1560, she was the widow of a Hungarian nobleman, Count Nadasay. She was brought to trial in 1611 after so many girls had vanished near her castle that the villagers demanded a search.

The governor of the province, her own cousin, the village priest and a number of soldiers raided the castle and arrested everyone inside. One girl was found in the hall, dead and drained of blood, and many others were shut in the dungeons.

The Countess, as close to a vampire as a real person can get, had, among other revolting practices, drunk their blood in the vain belief that this helped her complexion.

She refused to attend her trial, and because of her importance the lawyers were undecided how to punish her, though her servants were put to death. Finally, King Mathias of Hungary ordered her imprisonment in the castle, where she died three years later. The Lord Palatine described her as 'the blood-thirsty and blood-sucking Godless Woman'.

'A number of soldiers raided the castle and arrested everyone inside. One girl was found in the hall, dead and drained of blood, and many others were shut in the dungeons.'

Dracula – Prince Vlad V of Wallachia

There *was* such a person! He was a brave warrior and is considered a national hero in Romania today, but he was cruel even for his own time (1431–76). To give one example, he visited one of his strongholds and invited all the beggars in the town to a grand feast. Naturally they were overjoyed and crowded into the great hall. Then he locked the doors and set fire to the place. He explained that he wanted to reduce the risk of plague.

His enemies were the Turks and it is claimed that after one battle in 1456 he killed 20,000 of them. After another victory over the heathen Turk, the bells of Christendom rang out in rejoicing as far as the island of Rhodes. It was said that he made his state of Wallachia so safe that it was possible to leave a purse in the middle of the road and no one would touch or steal it. Probably no one *dared* to touch it!

In 1458, Vlad Dracula built the citadel of Bucharest, the present capital of Romania. His main headquarters were in Tirgoviste, where tourists are taken today on the *wrong* Dracula Tour (see Chapter 7) thinking they are going to see the landscape of Stoker's Count Dracula. It is well worth seeing all the same – the ruined battlements of Vlad's former palace dominated by a sixteenth-century tower with a magnificent view of the town, and flocks of schoolchildren below, in tunics of blue and white, listening while their teacher tells them about the glories of Vlad Dracula, if not the gore.

'He invited all the beggars in the town to a grand feast.
Naturally they were overjoyed and crowded into the great
hall. Then he locked the doors and set fire to the place.'

He was known in his day as Vlad the Impaler (Vlad Tepes, *tzepa* meaning spike) because he enjoyed impaling his enemies on tall stakes. An old print shows Vlad eating a meal beneath a row of impaled Turks as if it were the most natural thing in the world. When one of his men was rash enough to object to the screams and smells, Vlad had him impaled as well, on a higher stake, saying: 'You live up there, yonder, where the stench cannot reach you.'

To be fair to Vlad, the thousands of impaled bodies dotted across the countryside acted as a terrible warning to the Turks not to invade any further. There was a famous episode when a deputation of visiting ambassadors forgot to doff their turbans to Vlad in respect. He ordered the turbans should be nailed to their heads – a lesson in good manners to be copied later by Ivan the Terrible.

Was Vlad Dracula the model for Count Dracula? Some people think so, including members of the Dracula Society in London. As a matter of fact, there is a resemblance in the 1485 'Lubeck print' of Vlad to the 'thin nose and peculiarly arched nostrils', the 'heavy moustache' and 'the peculiarly sharp white teeth' that Stoker gives to the Count in the novel. He mentions some of the historical background too. That's as far as the resemblance goes, for Vlad was *not* a vampire.

Inset: A woodcut of Vlad V of Wallachia, known as the Impaler because of his particularly cruel method of executing his enemies.

Ivan the Terrible, Tsar of Russia

He lived from 1530 to 1584 and was given to fits of mad anger and prayerful repentance. In one of the former he murdered his eldest son. The young man was tactless enough to taunt his father over his losses abroad to the Poles. Ivan saw red – maybe literally – and struck his son again and again on the head with a heavy steel handle. With his last words, the young man forgave his father.

Ivan shared Vlad's love of torture. Once he attacked a castle for several days with cannon until the people inside decided on a last heroic act. They filled the vaults with gunpowder, and one of the defenders took a lighted torch to blow up the castle and everyone in it, so that they should not fall into Ivan's hands. There was a terrible explosion and everyone perished except for the man who started it. He lived for a short time but was dead when his blackened body was hoisted on a stake to be impaled. Ivan was so angry that he murdered all the inhabitants in the surrounding countryside, cutting them to bits or burning them alive. After such atrocities, there is no need to ask how he got his name!

Ivan the Terrible, Tsar of Russia, 1553–1584.

Rasputin

Grigori Yefimovich Rasputin (1872–1916) has been called 'the mad monk', 'the Holy Devil' and other such names. He has been portrayed as a wild peasant whose intrigues helped to bring about the downfall of Nicholas and Alexandra, the last Tsar and Tsarina of Russia.

Rasputin possessed remarkable powers of healing. As the Tsar's little boy suffered from haemophilia (a condition which makes it difficult to stop bleeding once it starts, so that even a scratch is dangerous), it is hardly surprising that the Tsarina was desperately anxious for any help Rasputin might offer.

Rasputin, 1871–1916. Rasputin exerted great influence over the Russian Court because the Tsarina thought that he could cure her son of haemophilia.

Was he so evil? Christopher Lee, who portrayed him in a film, thinks he has been 'much maligned'. So does Colin Wilson in his book *The Occult*. To start with, Wilson dismisses the claim that the very name 'Rasputin' means 'the dirty one' – 'if it did, he would no doubt have had the sense to change his name early in his career. It means "a crossroads", and happens to be as common as Smith in the village where he was born, Pokrovskoe.'

Perhaps people feared that Rasputin would use his influence politically, for he was murdered on 29th December, 1916. He was invited to a dinner party by Prince Yussipov, an aristocratic dandy. First he was given poisoned cakes, but these had no effect, possibly because he had been taking small amounts of cyanide for some time to make him immune. Then he was shot. As he staggered out of the house his attackers shot him again, terrified by his superhuman strength. Finally they beat him to death with an iron bar and stuck him under the ice in the River Neva that flows through St Petersburg, or Leningrad as it is now called. Even then, scratches were found on the ice where he had tried to crawl out before he died.

Rasputin left a letter in which he forecast his own death and prophesied the end of the Russian Royal family. He said that if he was killed by Russian noblemen, the Tsar and his family would lose the throne within two years. The Russian revolution took place the following year, and the Tsar, his wife and his children (with the possible exception of Anastasia) disappeared, and it is almost certain that they were executed in 1918.

Plainly Rasputin had extraordinary, almost hypnotic powers – but the evidence does not confirm that he was really the 'horror man' so often described.

Sawney Bean – the Scottish cannibal

You only have to fly over Scotland to realise how surprisingly unspoilt some parts remain, even today. Imagine what it would have been like in remote regions a few hundred years ago, and the sort of dangers a traveller might meet.

Sawney Bean was born a few kilometres outside Edinburgh, in the reign of James I of Scotland (1394–1437). His father was a hedger and ditcher, and Sawney tried this too, but tired of it quickly. He ran off to a lonely part of the countryside, the coast of Galloway, where he lived for the next twenty-five years. During this time, he had a large number of children by the woman he had taken with him, and they gave him an even larger number of grandchildren – not so much a family, as a clan. Their home was a series of caves by the shore. Their supplies came from robbing passing travellers, and their food from eating them.

Inset: Part of the Galloway coast where travellers were terrorised by the Bean family for twenty-five years.

The limbs of their victims were pickled, but at times they had so many that they threw them into the sea, as far from their caves as possible. When the tide washed up arms and legs along the coastline, people wondered who was guilty of such atrocities. As more and more travellers disappeared in this particular part of Scotland, the outcry grew.

Spies were sent out, but either they returned with nothing to tell, or they were never seen again. Innocent people were executed, and many moved away before they were suspected. The countryside became increasingly desolate.

Meanwhile, the vast Sawney Bean family flourished. They were careful never to attack more than two horsemen at a time, and surrounded these carefully so there was no chance of a rapid escape. Travellers on foot were easier game – four or five at a time were disposed of easily and dragged to their caves.

When the tide was high, the water came two hundred metres inside their cave, which stretched for nearly two kilometres. No one, seeing such a place, would believe that people could live there.

Then, as it was bound to, their luck ran out. A man and wife were returning on horseback from a country fair, when they were attacked in the usual manner. The ferocity was described by John Nicholson in his *Historical Tales connected with the South of Scotland* (1843):

'In the conflict the poor woman fell from behind him, and was instantly butchered before her husband's face, for the female cannibals cut her throat, and fell to sucking her blood with as great a gusto, as if it had been wine . . . Such a dreadful spectacle made the man make the more obstinate resistance, as he expected the same fate, if he fell into their hands.'

He fought back, and at that moment twenty or thirty men, also returning from the fair, arrived in time to rescue him. The man told them what had happened and showed them the body of his wife, which the Beans had dragged away and then abandoned. Shocked by their discovery, they took the man to Glasgow, where the magistrates instantly informed the King.

Four days later, the King set out in person with four hundred men, led by the only man who had survived such an attack by the cannibals. A team of bloodhounds went with them. Nothing was found. Even when they reached the mouth of the cave they could see nothing, and were continuing along the seashore when some of the hounds took up a scent and bounded inside. Immediately there was such a hideous howling that the soldiers turned back to investigate. All was darkness, but the hounds went deeper and deeper inside, refusing to come back as ordered. When the soldiers realised something or someone must be there, they sent for torches. They found dismembered bodies together with clothing, money, jewels and so on taken from the people whom the tribe had murdered.

They took all the remains they could find
and buried them in the sand. They seized
Sawney Bean, his wife, eight sons, six
daughters, eighteen grandsons and fourteen
granddaughters, and dragged them back to
Edinburgh for all the countryside to see – the
'cursed tribe' captured at last.

They were executed at Leith without trial –
it was not thought necessary. The men were
dismembered and the rest burnt to death. 'They
all in general died without the least sign of repentance, but continued cursing and vending
the most dreadful imprecations to the very last
gasp of life.'

139

The Stranglers of Bombay

The religious assassins who terrorised this region of India in the nineteenth century gave a name to the English language – *thug*. This is defined by the Oxford Dictionary as 'cut-throat, ruffian'. The Thugs were also called Phansigars ('phansis' meaning noose), for these were The Stranglers of Bombay.

They were unusual criminals – deeply religious and frequently respected members of the community who enjoyed killing. When they robbed travellers it was not so much the theft, as the strangulation that excited them, as they offered up their victims as sacrifices to the Hindu goddess Kali.

In his psychology of murder, *Order of Assassins*, Colin Wilson describes their cunning method of attack. They lived quietly for most of the year in their villages, causing no suspicion, but in winter they took to the roads, making sure they kept at least 150 kilometres from home. When they came across a group of travellers, one or two of the Thugs would approach and ask if they could join them for protection. A few days later some more Thugs would do the same. Soon there were more Thugs than travellers. They waited for an evening when the travellers were seated round the fire, then three Thugs would creep up behind each victim, and strangle him. It was all over in seconds. Then they hacked up the bodies so that they could not be identified. Now came the most important part for the Thugs – a private religious ceremony in which they prayed to Kali.

Sleeman was fascinated by the Thug atrocities and in 1829, when he revealed that they killed thousands of travellers every year, he caused a sensation both in India and back home in England. The next year Sleeman was given the job of suppressing them.

To begin with, the Thugs kept to a strict code of rules. Because Kali was a goddess, no woman was supposed to be killed, nor blind man, nor carpenter. There were several such exceptions, but eventually this became so tiresome to the Thugs that they grew greedy and careless and no one was safe. Soon, several of the Thugs were captured, and it was this sort of bungling compared to the careful precautions they used before, that proved their undoing. By 1850, 4,000 Thugs had been brought to trial, and their thuggery was over.

Colin Wilson is particularly interested in their compulsion to kill. They practised violence for the sake of violence, rather like the Manson killers of California in our time. He writes:

'This exciting game – of stalking and strangling human beings – became a drug, an addiction. This is what troubled the British investigators, who were ordinary soldiers and civil servants – men of the Dr Watson type. They sensed that the Thug murders were an inverted creative act, which brought its own peculiar deep satisfaction, and the thought made them shudder.'

The fact that they murdered in the name of religion does not make them any the less horrible. On the contrary, it makes them worse.

Jack the Ripper

His term of terror was short and swift and far from sweet. In 1888 he killed five women in six weeks, within a 'square mile' of London. While Count Dracula is so familiar that he seems almost human, the Ripper – who *was* real – has become a part of folklore.

His fame (one could almost say his popularity) is as fascinating as the murders he committed. He caused a panic throughout all of England at the time. Today, nearly a hundred years later, a new book is published about him almost every year, Scotland Yard receive several 'Ripper' letters a week, tourists are guided round his old murder sites in the East End, and plays, films and even musicals continue to make his name a household word.

Why is Jack the Ripper the most celebrated murderer in history? There is one obvious reason – he escaped. London police or 'Peelers' (some of them dressed up as women to act as decoys), voluntary 'vigilance' patrols, bloodhounds and journalists all searched for him in that small area, but he slipped past every time, in spite of bloodstains on his clothes.

Bucks Row, London, where Mary Ann Nicholls, one of the Ripper's victims, was found lying across the gutter.

The front page from the Sunday, November 17th, 1888, edition of the Illustrated Police News.

On one occasion, the night of a double murder, 30th September, it is probable that he was hiding in the yard where he had murdered a woman when a hawker drove in with his pony and trap and the animal shied at the smell of fresh blood. The hawker jumped down to see what was wrong, and discovered the corpse of Elizabeth Stride, blood still pouring from her throat. As he knelt beside her, the Ripper slipped away and vanished.

There have been other murderers who were never caught (like 'Jack the Stripper', who killed six women in 1964), but they never caused the same sensation. One reason for his exceptional notoriety is the flourish with which he signed himself when he wrote his macabre letters to the newspapers:

'How can they catch me now? I love my work and want to start again.

'You will soon hear of me and my funny little games. I saved some of the proper red stuff in a ginger beer bottle over the last job, to write with, but it went thick like glue and I can't use it. Red ink is fit enough I hope. Ha! Ha!

'The next job I do I shall clip the lady's ears off and send to the police officers just for jolly wouldn't you. Keep this letter back 'till I do a bit more work, then give it out straight.

'My knife is nice and sharp I want to get to work right away if I get a chance. Good luck.

Yours truly,
Jack the Ripper.'

Jack the Ripper – it was the perfect name! Alarming, memorable and deadly accurate, as police photographs of the victims prove.

But why did he cause such panic in 1888, when the East End of London was a sprawling, festering port, a melting-pot of nationalities where the cry of 'murder' was so common that people took no notice? Partly because murder *was* commonplace. The Ripper shone a spotlight on the dreadful conditions and poverty which people preferred to ignore, pretending they did not exist. He put an end to such pretence and shocked the conscience of the 'upper-classes'. Queen Victoria demanded an investigation and insisted on better street-lighting and clergymen thundered out sermons from their pulpits.

An American actor, Richard Mansfield, even withdrew his production at the Lyceum Theatre of *Dr Jekyll and Mr Hyde* because, as the *Daily Telegraph* put it, 'there is quite sufficient to make us shudder out of doors.' Ironically, Jack the Ripper was the greatest reformer the East End knew. Conditions were never so bad again.

But why did he kill? What was the nature of the murders? Was there a pattern? A motive? It seemed that the victims were chosen at random, and this was a terrifying thought, for it meant that no one was safe. Certainly he did not kill for money. Apart from his last victim, Mary Kelly, they were pathetic, middle-aged women who had come down in the world and stayed in dismal doss-houses.

But Mary Kelly was different – she was younger, prettier, and lived in a rented room of her own. It was noticed that the Ripper's

murders grew more ferocious every time, as if they were building up to a climax. The murder of Mary Kelly could hardly have been more horrible. Afterwards it is believed he slipped out to mingle with crowds who were starting to flock towards the Lord Mayor's Show.

A photographer took a close-up of Mary Kelly's eyes in the belief that the last image remains on the retina. This theory is described, brilliantly, in Rudyard Kipling's short story *At the End of the Passage* – but, of course, nothing was found. This was the end for the Commissioner of Police, Sir Charles Warren, whose resignation was greeted with cheers in the House of Commons. It was the end for the Ripper too. Either he had been searching for Mary Kelly in particular, had found her and had taken his revenge, or his blood-lust had worn itself out and he could go no further.

Who was Jack the Ripper? There is another reason why his name lives on – hunt the Ripper has become a national game in Britain. At first people imagined the Ripper to be a wild, black-bearded foreigner with a bagful of sharpened knives. Other suggestions include 'a Tsarist political agent', an eminent doctor, a midwife (Jill the Ripper), a mad poet, and – most colourful of all – the Duke of Clarence, heir to the British throne who died soon after the murders and was succeeded by his brother who became King George V. There is no real evidence to prove any man guilty.

Perhaps the closest we shall ever get is the evidence discovered by the author of this book, who has written about it previously (*Jack the Ripper* by Daniel Farson). I was staying with a friend in the north of Wales in 1959, and mentioned that I was preparing a television programme on the Ripper. Learning this, my hostess remarked, 'That's an extraordinary coincidence: my mother-in-law knows a lot about it, and we're seeing her this afternoon.' The Dowager Lady Aberconway, who died in 1975, was the daughter of Sir Melville Macnaghten. He was in charge of Scotland Yard after the murders and was responsible for completing the Ripper file. After his death, Lady Aberconway copied out his private notes and gave these to me, and in this way I learnt, for the first time, the name of the man the police suspected.

Left: The story of the exploits of Jack the Ripper held the front page into 1889. This is an artist's impression of Jack the Ripper from an 1889 edition of the Illustrated Police News.
Top: All sorts of people were suspected of being the Ripper – the most extraordinary, perhaps, was Queen Victoria's grandson, the Duke of Clarence.
Above: Sir Charles Warren. Sir Charles was forced to resign as Commissioner of Police because his force made so little progress in the Jack the Ripper affair.

Montague John Druitt was an unsuccessful barrister and schoolmaster, dismissed from his school at Blackheath in that autumn of 1888. He was not a doctor, as Macnaghten believed, but his father, uncle and cousin were all doctors. At one time his cousin had a surgery in the Minories – right in the Ripper district, no more than a minute's walk from Mitre Square where Catherine Eddowes was killed in the double murder of 30th September. Educated at Winchester and Oxford, he was an ace cricketer.

But why consider him guilty? Because he fits the pattern. He drowned himself in the Thames after the last murder, and this certainly fits the theory that the Ripper could go no further. There is evidence that he was suspected by his own brother, who informed the police, but they tried to 'hush it up' as far as possible. The 'vigilance' patrols were called off in 1889, with no reason given except that the Ripper had been found 'drowned in the Thames.' The great forensic expert and authority on the Ripper, the late Professor Francis Camps, was convinced of Druitt's guilt, 'I am sure this is the answer at last.'

Was Druitt mad? Sir Melville Macnaghten wrote '. . . after his awful glut (in Miller's Court, where Mary Kelly lived) his brain gave way altogether.' It is possible that the opposite happened, and that as he walked into the void of dawn, his brain trembled for a moment and he realised what he had done. He revealed this in papers left for his brother William, and then he took his own appalled and appalling life.

There is no absolute proof, and there probably never will be any, but it appears that M. J. Druitt is the person most likely to have been Jack the Ripper.

Sir Melville Macnaghten succeeded Sir Charles Warren at Scotland Yard. He believed that Montague John Druitt was the Ripper.

148

The Vampire Killer

All murder is horrible, and the only reason for singling out John George Haigh, in this century, is that some people believe he was a sort of vampire.

Basil Copper (in *The Vampire*) claims:

'Though it has long been a matter of dispute among medical circles, there is no doubt in my mind that John George Haigh was a vampire in the classical tradition, possibly the only true monster in this field in the twentieth century. By this, of course, I do not mean to imply that he was a vampire in the supernatural sense, but there is at least a strong suggestion that he needed to drink blood in order to refresh and sustain himself.'

When he was arrested, the *Daily Mirror* newspaper headlined a sensational story about a 'vampire killer', but he was better known as the 'acid bath murderer', for this was how he disposed of his victims. He liquidated, literally, nine people – or so he claimed.

The John Haigh case was one of the most sensational in the history of British crime. Here police are searching for clues in a factory at Crawley, Sussex, after the discovery of a few remains of the body of a wealthy widow which had survived immersion in an acid bath.
Inset: Further police investigations into the Haigh case led to this doll's hospital in Dawes Road, Fulham.

Haigh's childhood was strict; his parents described themselves as 'God's elect' and even rebuked a schoolmaster who loaned the boy a copy of *Treasure Island*. In spite of, or because of, this upbringing, he started a life of petty fraud at an early age. When he was released from Lincoln Prison in the war, he was involved in a car crash:

'Blood poured from my head and down my face and into my mouth. This revived in me the taste (for blood) and that night I experienced another awful dream. I saw before me a forest of crucifixes, which gradually turned into trees. At first there appeared to be dew, or rain dripping from the branches but as I approached I realised it was blood. Suddenly the whole forest began to writhe and the trees, stark and erect, to ooze blood. A man went up to each tree catching the blood. When the cup was full he approached me. "Drink," he said, but I was unable to move and the dream faded.'

This is an extraordinary parallel to *The Death of Halpin Frayser*, a short story by Ambrose Bierce (see Chapter 4).

The fantasies Haigh told at his trial could have been a deliberate lie in the hope of being found 'guilty, but insane', but even if this was calculated, he was no more sane that Elizabeth Bathory, Jack the Ripper or even Vlad Tepes. Certainly he had no conscience. He referred to his arrest as 'this pickle', and looked forward to the trial ('it should be fun'). John George Haigh, the 'vampire killer' and acid bath murderer', was hanged in 1949.

John George Haigh, 1909–1949, the acid bath murderer and 'vampire killer'. Haigh bequeathed his green hopsack suit, green socks and red tie to dress this portrait in the Chamber of Horrors at Madame Tussaud's, London.

Postscript

*'The children have
never fallen for my nonsense!'*
(Boris Karloff)

Index

Acknowledgements

Beevor Collection 59; Camera Press (Text and Illustrations), London: Flipot-Zoot 154–155, George F. Trost 122, 123; W. F. Davidson 8–9, 136; Dracula Society 120, 121, 121 inset; Edinburgh City Library 18 left; Mary Evans Picture Library, London 24, 39, 62 left, 130 inset, 135, 147 top, 147 bottom, 148; Daniel Farson 74; Alan Frank 92–93; Colin Godman 10; The Ronald Grant Archive 96, 143; Rosemary Grimble 114 bottom, 115 top; Hamlyn Group: John Howard 23 inset, John Webb 153 inset; Hammer Films 22–23; Irish Tourist Board 75; Keystone Press Agency Ltd, London 28, 103; Kobal Collection, London endpapers, contents page, 86 left, 86 right, 90–91, 91 inset, 95 inset, 106 top, 106 bottom, 107; Madame Tussaud's, London 153 inset; The Mansell Collection, London 38, 58, 62 right, 80, 102, 134; John Murray (Publishers) Ltd 54; National Portrait Gallery, London 48, 52; Popperfoto, London 150, 150–151, 151 inset; Radio Times Hulton Picture Library, London 66, 67, 82, 111, 142, 146: Stills Library/National Film Archive, London 87, 95, 154 inset; The Sutcliffe Gallery, Whitby 118–119; ZEFA Picture Library, London: G. E. Mabbs title page; George G. Harrap & Company Limited, London 59 right.